I0575738

A Fowl Match

SARAH MADELINE

Copyright © 2025 by Sarah Madeline

All rights reserved.

No part of this novel may be reproduced in any form or by any means, including photocopying, recording, or other electronic or mechanical methods, without the prior written permission of the author, except for the use of brief quotations in a book review.

This is a work of fiction. The story, all names, organizations, characters, and incidents portrayed in this novel are either products of the author's imagination or are used fictitiously. No identification with actual persons (living or deceased), places, buildings, and products is intended or should be inferred.

ISBN 979-8-9928360-0-4

First edition: 2025

For my brother Ray, I miss you more than words can describe. You brought so much laughter and light into this world.

For anyone grieving someone they lost, I hope you know it's okay to be struggling. It's also okay to laugh and enjoy life too. They would want that for you. For your heart will always hold a piece of them.

Thornwood Valley

Green House

Thornwood Valley Park

Ice cream

NSSG The Laundry Basket The Olive Bean The Post Office The Hoarder Emporium The Chop Shop Bobbie's Freeze

Parking

The Cozy Cottage Retirement Home The Valley Harvest Cats & Novels Dr. Paula Newma

Thornwood Cabins

Hiking Trails

Chicken Coop

Valley Pond

Annie's Diner

The String Cheese

Chloe's Closet

Rooster's

The Cozy Cabin Inn

Fix-Its

Dan's Auto

Stop and Fill

Suds in the Bucket

The Rhett Family Farm

Chapter 1

VIOLET

I f I've learned anything in my past twenty-eight years of existence, it's the fact that I am a total klutz. You may be wondering, why did I think today would be any different? Your guess is as good as mine.

A gust of wind blows strands of hair all around my face, which is the last thing I need right now. I am trying my best to focus. I know this *could* end badly. No—this *will* end badly.

Steady, Violet.

I try to peek over the towering stack of eclectic pots piled in my arms. The effort is almost pointless. I only have myself to blame. I bargained a deal for five dollars and a bouquet of flowers, knowing I had more than enough planting pots in my flower and garden shop. So, now I'm walking down the sidewalk balancing stone, plastic, and terracotta pots on my arms. They wobble with every painstaking step I take. I even could have gone home to grab a box to put them in. What can I say, bad decisions were made.

I tend to make them a lot.

A small opening between two of the pots leaves a tiny line of sight, almost as if I'm trying to look through a microscopic gap.

This was a horrible idea.

To be fair, I couldn't refuse the deal Jane let them go for. She insisted I take some extras to help clear out her antique shop, The Hoarder's Emporium, a business in our small town of Thornwood Valley. But the amount I took wouldn't make a dent in reducing the stock. Her shop is overflowing with treasures and unique items. She's a vagabond who travels the continental U.S. once a month in her 1980s VW van.

A stone pot on the top of the stack sparkles in the sun and reflects the perfect amount on my face. My vision becomes blurry with the sudden burst that renders my eyes utterly useless. All I can see are grainy spots. I slow my pace to a stop, hoping to clear my eyes before things go south.

When I think things can't get any worse, they do.

My sneakers catch the joint of the sidewalk that dips down from the next square. The saying, "Step on a crack and break your mother's back," never felt true until today. Now, it's more like breaking my own back. Or maybe I'm entering a portal into a different realm, like the folklore suggests.

I tumble down. I squeeze the pots to my chest, hoping for the best.

As If I could fall gracefully.

Everything happens in slow motion. The pots go airborne like launched rockets. Some disappear to depths so far, it's hard to tell where they land. Each one a perfect symphony of fireworks shooting through the sky. My body continues downward. Every second that passes feels never-ending.

Stupid gravity.

As I become one with the ground, I hear a clunking noise and a deep grumble. I register it, but I have too much going on to wonder what that's about. Thankfully, the remaining pots break my fall. Although, it would have felt better if I was carrying a stack of pillows or something that could have cushioned the blow.

My gratitude is short-lived. The pressure of my body weight makes them shatter into a million pieces, emitting a crunching noise loud enough for the whole town to hear.

This is great. I might die of embarrassment.

Thornwood Valley is not a big city. Anything that goes on here is bound to hit the local news. Especially considering there is a dedicated social media page for the town. This will be the latest gossip for a few days.

"What the hell?" a deep voice grumbles from a few feet ahead of me.

I try my best to make out the man whose voice rang through my ears—one that was not too pleasant, if I must admit. But I don't recognize it. At this moment in time, I can't trust my judgment either. The ringing in my ears is perpetual.

I lay on the ground in defeat covered in shambles of broken pieces. Tiny bits of color litter around me, looking like the inside of a kaleidoscope. A stunning tragedy of a rainbow.

A tall shadow towers over me. I can see the large inky outline on the sidewalk from the corner of my eye. Sighing, I look up from the ground hesitantly.

It's time to accept my fate.

I peek over the battlefield, inching my chin higher and higher at small increments. I'm just prolonging my inevitable embarrassment. Hopefully, whoever is in front of me is someone I don't recognize. The chances of that are slim, but not entirely impossible. A few tourists are already in town for hiking trips.

As I look up, I notice a pair of shiny black dress shoes; I can almost make out my reflection looking back at me. I keep my gaze moving upward along slate gray dress slacks. They are crisply ironed. Strong arms cross over a broad chest. I can't help but feel a twinge of self-consciousness when my eyes meet his piercing stare. His cold blue gaze makes me feel exposed yet enthralled. They are the lightest blue, almost appearing to have a gray glimmer in the sunlight. His clean shaved face is angular and well-defined. His slightly crooked nose is the only part of his appearance that isn't *perfect*. And still, the way that it suits his face makes him exude masculinity. It's perfectly imperfect. Everything about him screams confidence. Or maybe it's self-assurance that radiates off him in waves.

The way he stands like a statue towering over me makes me feel so much shorter than I thought I was. I'm a modest five foot five and used to being one of the shortest people in a room. And yet I've never truly felt so small compared to someone else. It could be the fact that I'm lying on the ground. And he is standing. He's gotta be at least six feet.

Speaking of lying on the ground, I need to get up! I've been staring *way* too long. This thought makes me blush crimson.

I am mortified.

"Are you okay?" his deep voice murmurs. He reaches a hand out to help me up. I can almost make out a look of concern marred on his otherworldly features. I am absolutely lost in his gaze. I look from his outstretched hand and back to his eyes. Willing myself to take his hand in assistance, I do so reluctantly. I grasp his hand loosely as his fingers latch mine.

He tugs me straight up in one swift motion as if I weigh nothing. It takes the breath right out of my chest. I sway on my feet, willing them to stay planted on the ground. His fingers are still locked with mine. They steady me in place so I'm grounded to the spot.

I'm speechless, willing my brain for any semblance of a thought. *Nothing. I can't think of one thing to say.*

His eyes continue to search mine—waiting—probably looking for some sort of sign that I'm okay. Oh, that's right, he asked me a question!

Speak Violet. Say something to the handsome stranger or he will think you're crazy.

He probably already thinks that.

"I'm alright. Thank you." My voice sounds scratchy and quiet. The white lie feels bitter on my tongue—I'm the furthest from okay right now. It's not because of my massive fall or the shambles of the once beautiful pots, though. I'm used to falling on flat surfaces, leaving damage in my wake. It's the presence of the man before me that has me scatterbrained.

"Are you sure? You don't seem okay." He looks perplexed. "Maybe next time you should try and watch where you're going. You hit me in the head with one of those pots."

So that's what that clunking noise was. Stupid. Stupid. Stupid. Why do I always make bad decisions? "I'm so sorry! Are *you* okay? Do you need to see a doctor?" I fire off questions sporadically, hoping I didn't give him a concussion with that hit. It was a hard one, because those things shot through the air. "I can take you over to Dr. Newman. Her practice is right across the street. She can check you out and make sure you're okay."

"No doctor. I'm all good. It was one of the plastic ones. You shouldn't have been carrying that many anyway." He sighs, looking down at our hands. I didn't realize I was still holding his hand.

His expression changes and he suddenly releases my grasp. The warm embrace dissipates from my shaky hand, leaving it cold and empty. He appears to have come to an internal decision that I'm fine. His nonchalant shrug and spin away is enough of a sign. Then he continues down the sidewalk as if nothing occurred between us.

I look down at my feet and the pots surrounding me. "Wait a minute!" I jog down the sidewalk after him. "Can I buy you a drink or something? I owe you an apology."

He turns back as I catch up to him, out of breath. "No worries, honestly, there's no reason to apologize. Although the offer is tempting, I have too much going on today to stop for a drink."

In my mind that translates to, *I'd rather do anything else that doesn't involve you.*

"Oh, well, I hope you have a good day!"

One of his eyebrows goes up. "You too, Miss."

Miss? Do I look like a Miss to him? I guess he's more interested in running away than knowing my actual name.

As he retreats, I can't help but notice his gray suit and dress shoes again. They look so out of place. It makes me wonder who he really is. He isn't from here. I would have recognized him. And to forget a guy as enthralling as him, *no way*. Maybe he's a local that I've just never met? Or a tourist showing up? He doesn't look the type to go hiking, especially being in a suit, but what do I know. I guess I'll never find out.

I collect the broken pieces littering the ground and throw them in the trash, saving the few pots that survived to bring back to The Not So Secret Garden (NSSG), my shop.

"Thanks for the help, Grumpy," I mutter under my breath sarcastically at his retreating form. I breathe a sigh of relief and suddenly feel a bit better. One that I seem to have been holding onto throughout our entire interaction.

Chapter 2

DUSTIN

"What the hell?" I grumble.

I slap my hand against the nightstand with my eyes still closed. I need to shut off the annoying ass sound. It continues a crescendo.

Bang. Bang. Bang.

In my sleep haze my eyes flicker open. Through my blurred vision I stare at my phone screen. Four thirty in the morning. The noise isn't coming from my phone. It's coming from the front door.

That's when my surroundings come into view. And it hit's me hard. I'm on the farm, not in my apartment in New York City.

I flip over the cover and drag my feet across the carpet, down a few steps to the front door. I open it, the dark sky filters through the gap.

"Get the hell up, the day started thirty minutes ago. The goat's need milking, fed, and fresh water. If you want this responsibility, you better start showing some initiative." My grandpa says.

"Yes sir," I yawn.

"Five minutes. I'm giving you that long and nothing more. I'll be waiting outside in the side-by-side."

"Okay." I manage to say.

How did I end up in this predicament?

I grab a pair of jeans and t-shirt, shrugging them on. A flashback runs through my mind from five days ago, reminding me of how I ended up here.

"Hello?—Hello?—Dustin—it's good to hear—voice. How are you?—been a long time—I've heard from you." My grandpa's voice escapes the phone between each break of static. The cut in service makes it hard to decipher what he's conveying, especially at this hour.

"Umm—you know it's six a.m. on a Sunday, right Grandpa? Could we talk later when I'm awake? And alive?" I sandwich my head under a pillow to block out the blinding rays.

"It's six a.m. like I always say—"

"If you aren't up before the roosters crow you aren't up early enough."

"Exactly, I heard them crowing hours ago."

"You don't even have any chickens."

"That doesn't matter, you get my point."

"Yes, Sir." My voice comes out muffled from underneath the pillow.

"Anyways, this can't wait. We've waited long enough for you to take some responsibility. The farm needs your help. I need your help." His voice cracks on the I.

I open the front door and hop into the seat. He reverses and drives towards the goat's barn. We're silent for a few minutes, nothing but the rumble of the engine and gravel under the tires.

"Will you let me put a booster on your roof? My phone barely works out here."

He lets out a dry laugh, "Absolutely not. The day you put that high tech equipment in my home is the day I die."

I sigh. My hands are tied. I change the subject. "What's on the agenda for today?"

"Well, first off there's no agendas out here. You're not working in the office anymore."

"Thanks for the reminder." It's still raw. The reminder of being laid off doesn't sit well in my empty stomach.

He continues as we pull in front of the goat barn, "we'll take care of the goats. There is a lot of things you need to learn. Since we didn't have them when you were younger. Then off to mucking the cow barn. But, you've got that handled on your own. You've done that plenty of times before."

"Yeah, I'm good with that." There goes my brand new clothes I bought yesterday. I rub my head at the reminder. It still stings a little where I got hit on the head.

"And then we'll check the fences. I'm sure there are a few spots that need to be re-strung. Those nasty windstorms did some damage. It won't get done all in one day. But you can get a head start."

"Anything else?"

"Plenty, but we don't have enough time in the day to sit here and talk. Let's get to work."

After a few grueling hours of milking goats and feeding. Filling water troughs, laying down fresh hay. My grandfather dropped me off in front of the cattle barn.

The grueling part had nothing to do with milking or goats. No, it had to do with my grandfather's agitation with *me*. I can sense some hostility that can only be rebuilt through time. Lots of time.

I shovel cow manure into the spreader on the back of the tractor using the skid steer. With each scoop my nose stings with the smell. I'm not used to it, after not being here for years. I've gotten acclimated to the odor of garbage, car exhausts, and a variety of fumes. Some pleasant, others not so much. The same can be said for life on the farm.

Once the spreader is full, I drive it across the field. I shift the tractor into a higher gear, it grinds with each movement. Shooting manure all over the new growth. I repeat this process multiple times until the section of field is covered, and I can see the concrete floor of the barn. I shovel the rest of the concrete where I couldn't get the skid steer. I hose the floor down and scrub it clean. Hours later I wipe my brow, entirely exhausted after a full day of manual labor. Being a farmer is no easy feat. As I stand here and look at what I've accomplished, I feel pride in my chest. After sitting at a desk for years as an accountant, the change of pace feels refreshing.

I peek out the barn doors, the sky is bright red with wisps of orange and purple. Cows graze the field surrounding me, goats on the other side. The landscape is never ending. Nothing in sight but the barns, pastures, and trees. My A-Frame and the farmhouse are a blip in the grand scheme of things.

I missed the slow pace of this life.

I walk in the back door of my grandparents' farmhouse. After scrubbing my skin raw for the past hour, I'm ready for dinner. I don't have the energy to make myself something. But why would I? My grandma makes the best food.

"Oh, my dear!" My grandmother places her palm over her heart. "I still can't believe you're here." She pulls me into a bone-crushing embrace.

"I saw you yesterday, we've already done this." She holds onto me for what feels like hours. "You can let go now. I can't breathe."

"I know. But it still doesn't feel real. I don't want to let go. I'm afraid you'll disappear again."

"Oh grandma, I'm not going anywhere," I assure her. At least not for the next couple of months. Until I decide on whether I want to stay here permanently.

"I'll believe that when I see it." My grandfather grunts under his breath.

"I missed you too Grandpa. Haven't I shown you that I'm serious about staying for a while. Look what I accomplished today."

"If you did then you would have come back here sooner. It was one day of work. We'll see after you spend a week working." I can tell my grandfather still holds a grudge for my not returning. I can't blame him. He's been holding it through yesterday and today. And he will for weeks to come. He doesn't let things go easily.

A knock on the door sounds.

"Who's that?" I ask.

"That's Mason, he was coming by to buy some goat's cheese," my grandma says.

"I'll get it." The door creaks on its hinges as I open it.

"Dustin. It's good to see you man." Mason claps me on the shoulder in greeting.

"What's it been? Twelve years?"

"Feels more like twenty, but who's counting?" He chuckles. "I heard you were back in town, but I didn't believe it. Now that

I'm seeing you with my own two eyes, the whispers must be true. Unless I need a new prescription for these damn glasses."

"You better believe it's me."

"Last I heard you were living in the city. In some high-rise apartment making the big bucks."

I amiably elbow him in the arm. "Last I heard you took over Rooster's Bar and were making the big bucks."

"Fair Point." Mason's cheeks rise in a grin. "It's good to see you back on the farm again. I remember the days when I used to help out in high school while you were here for the summers." We both walk to his F-150 truck. Mason releases the tailgate to reveal a large cooler.

"How could I forget? We were always getting in trouble." I chuckle at the thought. "So, what's the cheese for?"

"For the big night; the special is goat's cheeseburgers."

"What does this big night entail?" My eyebrows absent-mindedly rise in question.

"The Thornwood Valley Heartbreakers of course."

"They're still a thing?" I ask, reminiscing on the nights my grandparents used to take me to listen to the band play cover songs. My parents would have been so pissed off if they knew I used to go to the bar when I was younger. It was the highlight of my summer—the live music, chitter-chatter, and thrill of doing something I wasn't allowed.

"Yep. And they are better than ever. Everyone is coming out tomorrow so I'm hoping for a successful night of sales. You should stop by to have a drink and a burger, on me. Listen to them for old time's sake."

"God, we sound like two codgers reminiscing."

"That's because we are."

"We're thirty, not senile," I say as I follow Mason to the industrial fridge to help carry the cheese. "I think I'll take you up on that offer. I've got nothing else better to do."

Chapter 3

VIOLET

I check my reflection one last time in the mirror, then finger comb my hair to the ends a little past my shoulders to make sure I didn't miss any tangles. My face is makeup free, like usual. Bootcut jeans cling to my thighs and drape out at my feet. I sport a pair of hiking boots and a sage green crewneck.

Don't judge me; I strive for comfort!

It's weird to be getting ready to go out. It's been so long since I've let myself have any free time to do anything remotely exciting outside of work.

I rush down the stairs of my apartment that's above my shop to find Olive, my best friend, standing at the front door. She looks rather impatient tapping her suede high top boots. I can't blame her. I'm late yet again.

Her appearance is completely different from mine. Natural red curls flow from her shoulders. Her lips are painted burgundy, a striking contrast against her pale skin. She wears black skinny jeans and a distressed jean jacket.

"You look amazing, Olive!" I say.

"You do too! Now let's go. We don't want to miss the first song." She grabs my hand and tugs me out onto the sidewalk, dragging me along.

The air outside is extremely chilly. The nights are still cold, while the days are starting to warm. It sends a shiver that courses through my body, enticing goosebumps to prickle on my arms and legs.

The walk to Rooster's Bar is short. Only a few shops down the sidewalk. The whole town is in one long strip. A straight line of shops on either side of the road. Every store you could think of that has exactly what you need is right here. There isn't much variety, but enough that I don't have to leave town for anything. Surrounded by a pond, park, trails, and the Thornwood Cabins, the town is perfect for anyone. On either side the hills slope up.

"Aren't you so excited to hear them play? I heard they have a new line up of cover songs that they will be playing for the first time tonight."

"Yes! I've been wanting to hear their new covers. I haven't had the time to go," I admit.

At a rather fast pace we pass a bunch of small shops on the left of the street. The Laundry Basket, The Olive Bean, The Hoarders Emporium, The Chop Shop, Bobbie's Freeze. Then there's Annie's Diner, The String Cheese—which has the best pepperoni rolls I've ever eaten in my life—and Chloe's Closet. There's also a bunch of other shops on the right side of the street, each one bursting at the seams with character. Colorful storefronts are mostly converted homes that reflect the personality of the owners.

Rooster's Bar is nearly the last place on the street. You would never guess what Rooster's is named after.

A Rooster!

The town's late Rooster the Rooster. Yeah, that's right. Named after a chicken that has since passed on and a new rooster took its place a few years back. Although, the name isn't very original. Mason, the bar's owner, has a flock of twenty or so chickens that roam the town during the day. They are locked up at night in the coop that's pretty far behind the bar. This keeps them safe from racoons, hawks, and foxes that are common predators in the area.

He had a flock penned up for a while until one day they escaped. The town folks loved interacting with the chickens so much they begged him to let them roam free. He has ever since. The tourists love hanging out with the chickens as well, so it's a win-win. Except for one teensy problem.

The chicken shit.

As a business owner I try to keep the front sidewalk clean and welcoming. It's the first impression any customer gets of whether they will enter the store or not. Well, the chickens like to poop all over the concrete. Only some days, though, but no—I'm lying.

Every day.

So, it adds more work for me and the other business owners to keep a clean storefront. But, who am I kidding, I love them. It's worth the extra clean up. Once a week we rotate who pressure washes the sidewalks to keep them looking nice and clean.

There's even a bench in front of the bar with a remembrance plaque in honor of the late rooster. People buy flowers from my shop to place in front of it weekly in his memory. It's become a tradition.

To top it all off Chloe's Closet, the town's clothing store, has a section dedicated to Rooster. Shirts, sweatshirts, crewnecks and more branded clothing with Rooster and his hens on the front. Remember that sage green sweatshirt I put on earlier? Yeah, he's there right on the front of it.

And you may be thinking, Aren't roosters mean? Nope. Not this rooster. He is the most docile one I've ever encountered. With beautiful black and white feathers. He's a Barred Plymouth Rock. Although, his hens are all different breeds. Plymouth Rocks, Americanas, California Whites, Rhode Island Reds, Silkies, and Brahmas. Each different breed of chicken lays different colored eggs, making for a variety of colors: green, brown, and white eggs. Each one has a different shape and size. They add to the charm of the town. Every chicken is unique, and this keeps them from picking on each other.

"Cut it out," Olive says, snapping her fingers in front of my face.

I jump at the sudden realization that we are already here. I was lost in my thoughts. "Oops! Sorry, I was thinking about Rooster and his girls."

She chuckles and we walk into the lit-up bar. "Of course you are! I could tell you didn't hear a word I was saying."

"Sorry!" I softly smile and enter the booming bar.

Chapter 4

VIOLET

The bar is extremely packed for a Friday night. It must be because of the new set the Thornwood Heartbreakers are playing.

I recognize almost every face I see. All small-town folks. Farmers finished from a long day of work, the small business owners from the strip of town, blue collar workers, and almost everyone else that lives in the surrounding properties. A few tourists are here also. When the weather gets a little warmer more of them start rolling in for hiking trips, camping, and fishing. So, we all try to enjoy the time the town is empty when we can relax before the influx of people.

As we make our way closer to the bar, there are only two empty seats left. And they are not directly next to each other. A man sits in the middle. So, Olive and I will most likely be split up. All of the round oak tables that line the center between the bar and stage are filled. Once the night goes on some townies dance in front of the stage and tables.

The bar is decorated in a rustic theme. A live edge counter coated in epoxy follows the left wall. Recessed lighting shades the inside in a warm glow. Assorted bottles of alcohol are neatly arranged on a few shelves behind the counter. Vintage tin signs hang all over the establishment, some with coca cola, betty boop, and corona. Adorning the walls with accents of color that pop against the dark wood paneled walls. Glasses clink and drip with condensation. The faint aroma of smoke and beer lingers in the air.

"Well, this sucks," Olive says as we make it to the black leather stools. The man sitting in the center is someone I don't think I've met before. He is tall, that much I can tell even though he's sitting. His boots hit the floor, where mine normally dangle high above the stone, tiled floor when sitting on the stools. His hair is short and brown with streaks of natural dirty blonde. He's dressed in a pair of dark jeans and a forest green and white striped flannel. I'm not sure who he is because I can't see his face.

"Who's that?" I whisper in Olive's ear.

"Who? Him?" she shouts over the chatter and points directly at him.

I tug on her arm, pressing my pointer finger against my lips. "Shhhh. Yes, I don't recognize him."

"Oh, I have no clue who that is." She giggles, whispering this time, "Isn't he dreamy?"

I don't know if he's dreamy. How would she know? He hasn't turned around yet.

"Are you already drunk?" I ask. "You are too giggly, and you haven't even had a sip yet."

"I may have prepared before we came." She winks.

Oh no. Here we go again.

She makes bad decisions when drinking. Normally involving guys. Hopefully Chad isn't here. He's her ex-boyfriend. And he is notorious for breaking her heart.

"Okay, I'm gonna ask if he will move down a stool so that we can sit together," I say as I grab her arm, "Stay here, okay?"

"Yes ma'am." She hiccups.

I roll my eyes and approach the mystery man. I tap him on the shoulder, and he looks at me. And that's when it clicks. I've met him before. A memory flashes in my mind of a few days earlier.

Mr. Grumpy.

Olive was right, he is dreamy. I understand all too well. I am utterly speechless again.

"Yes?—you again," he grumbles, his husky voice laced with annoyance once he recognizes me.

Boy, do I regret touching him. I think I poked a bear. He scowls, eyebrows furrowed in a disapproving glare. And the instant attraction I felt towards him fades away—yet again. As for my willingness to be friendly and swoon.

"Who's been peeing in his wheaties?" I think to myself but whisper out loud without control.

"Excuse me?" He crosses his strong arms over his chest, looking even more annoyed.

Oh! I cover my mouth with my hand.

"Oh crap. Did I say that out loud?"

"Yep. Indeed, you did. What do you want?"

Hmmm. Okay. I get it. He's not a happy camper.

I didn't mean to go blurting my inner thoughts. I meant to keep that thought shoved away. Deep in the confines of my mind.

But it's too late now to take it back. Maybe I should roll with it?

"Look, my friend and I showed up late and we wanted to sit next to each other. I point to Olive standing behind me and she gives a pearly white smile, all her teeth on display, and a wave. "Would you be able to move down a seat so that we aren't separated? *Please*. If you don't mind? I didn't mean to bother you again. And I'm so sorry about hitting you in the head." I ask as nicely as I can, feeling slightly bad for disturbing him and saying that comment aloud. Kill with kindness, right?

"I do mind, actually. I was here first. And I happen to like sitting here. It's the best view of the stage."

So that's how it's going to be. Two can play at this game.

"Are we twelve? 'I was here first.' I haven't heard that one since middle school. And is one stool down going to block your view of the stage? I don't think so."

"Whatever you want to think, *darling.*"

Darling? I am not anyone's *darling*. First, he calls me Miss, now I'm darling! What's it going to be next? I don't think the next one is going to be a nice term of endearment.

I've come to the conclusion that he is a gigantic jerk. And this will not end well.

Tonight, I will end up doing one of two things: making my one phone call to Olive, while at the police department, begging her to bail me out. Or two, punching this guy straight in his smug face. I hope the latter, but both could actually happen, I realize.

I need to be civil; we are here for a good time. It's not like I want to choose violence. Or have these negative thoughts. That's normally Olive's forte. What has gotten into me? Something about his instant scowl set me off.

"Hey Olive, Mr. Grumpy won't move. So, I guess we have to be separated," I say loud enough so he can hear.

"I don't care as long as I can order a drink," she says and waves over the bartender, ordering a whiskey neat. The bartender/owner, Mason, knows my order so I don't have to say anything. I never stray from my usual, while Olive likes to change up her order every time. Mason smiles at me and starts making our drinks.

I sit at the bar, sliding my fingers across the smooth wood grain surface. The lights are bright in here, but the dark walls make it a relaxing environment. Sounds start to travel from the stage, announcing the band's first song.

The microphone whizzes and the sounds of someone tapping on it fills the bar. The chatter of the once loud environment dies down. "Ahhem, thank you all for being here to hear our new set. The first cover we're going to play is 'Drinkin' my baby (off my mind)' by Eddie Rabbitt." The singer's voice sounds across the bar with melancholy. Mason slides my beverage towards me across the bar.

"One mocktail for Vivi and a whiskey neat for Olive."

"Thanks Mason. How's business?" I ask.

"No problem. Anything for you." He wipes the counter off with a rag. "The last couple weekends have been packed so I'm hiring a couple more employees. The Heartbreakers have been bringing in a ton of customers lately."

"Call me or stop by if you need any help before you find someone."

"You're the best. I might need you next weekend if I can't find anyone by then."

"Mason!" Olive calls, trying to get his attention before I can answer.

"Olive!" He shakes his head and shoots her a grin.

"I'm making some strawberry pop tarts on Monday as a test. I want to perfect them before I add it to the breakfast menu. If you stop by in the morning, you can be my test subject."

"I'll be there, no doubts about it. My stomach is already grumbling."

"Hey! Where's my invite? Are we not best friends anymore?" I tease Olive, knowing all too well I'm not about to miss out on her pastries. Her coffee shop, The Olive Bean, is a daily stop before I open for the day. It keeps me sane.

"Well, you would've known you were already invited if you listened to me on the walk here. You were in a bubble thinking about the chickens, remember? I had a full-on conversation with myself."

"Oops, sorry Olive, I'll be there."

"Good." She nudges Grumpy with her elbow, and he grunts in response while turning his gaze to her. "You want to join us on Friday at the Olive Bean a half hour before I open? Strawberry Poptarts." She wiggles her eyebrows up and down.

"I don't know."

"Come on. They'll be delicious. Hopefully. I can always use a few more opinions."

"Okay. I'll stop by for a few minutes."

I glare at Olive, and she winks at me.

"See you guys Friday," Mason says and then turns towards someone looking for a drink.

The sounds from the song flicker through my ears. It soothes my agitation caused by my companion next to me. Until he speaks again.

"Mocktail? Are you a square?"

That's it, I will be in jail tonight!

"Does it look like I'm a square?" I ask, bewildered someone could even possibly utter something so disrespectful and judgmental, and *lack* manners. "Wait, don't even answer that question," I say huffing while taking a sip of the sweet goodness.

He chuckles. I'd love to swipe that smug grin off his face. "I mean that chicken sweatshirt screams it."

"I hope the rooster leaves a surprise on him," I mumble under my breath.

"What was that?"

"Oh I was saying how I'm the squarest square of all. Ninety-degree corners and all. So boring. You shouldn't talk to me, you might fall asleep from all the fuddy-duddy emanating from me."

Yep, that was the worst comeback I have ever thought of.

"Ha. Okay, *fuddy-duddy*," he says while leaning back on the bar stool.

"Okay, Wade Walker."

"Who's Wade and what does he have to do with this?" He scruffs his short hair, looking perplexed.

"Wade Walker from the movie *Cry-Baby*. Only the greatest 90s movie of all time." I pause to contain my astonishment. "You called me a square like the drapes and squares in the movie; that's what he has to do with this."

"Never heard of it." He takes a sip of his drink.

Another red flag in my book.

The band plays a few more songs, "Fishin' in the dark" by The Nitty Gritty Dirt Band, "I fall to pieces" by Patsy Cline, "Ring of Fire" by Johnny Cash. People dance, sing and sway to the soothing melodies. The band sounds amazing. And I am having a great time. Olive is dancing with Mason in front of the stage. He twirls her around to the thrumming sounds. Her hair swooshes in a cloud around them.

They have been good friends for years and I always wondered when they would become something more than friends. But at the moment I don't think Olive notices how Mason looks at her.

I'm getting ready to leave as the last song plays when I see Constance at the microphone. I widen my eyes.

This has to be good.

Constance, Chuck's wife, is Thornwood Valley's gossip executive—yes, that's what she refers to herself as. She feels it's her job (self-appointed), since no one else has any interest in keeping the town updated with things that go on. Every small town has someone that is in charge of spreading the word about all of the gossip and happenings. She was the one to fill the position. Constance runs the town's events and is part of the gossip mill.

She also owns The Chop Shop, the town's only barber shop. The business was inherited from her parents when she graduated high school. Chelsea, her daughter, now runs the place and continues their legacy. Bobbie and Annie are the other two parts of her trio. They meet twice a week updating each other with the comings and goings of the town. They aren't mean spirited, but they will find out all of your secrets and make them public knowledge. They like to involve themselves in matchmaking, events, and anything that happens.

Secrets are hard to keep in our small town.

"Hi everyone, I hope you had a good time tonight. I have an exciting announcement before you leave." Constance brushes an imaginary piece of lint from her floral dress and continues, "As you all know, starting Monday the town's annual spring festival month starts. And it's a special one, the twentieth anniversary since the first one ever celebrated in our quaint town. That means it's time for everyone to be partnered up in groups of two. Each group will team together to participate in all of the events."

How could I have forgotten? Every year this happens in the first week of March. The events commence. And every business owner is entered into a bucket that is drawn at random. We are all pulled in groups of two to compete with the other teams. It raises money for all of the small businesses. Tourists come to our town to watch the festivities and participate in games set up. They stay in the cabins and at the Cozy Cabin Inn. Some town folks also bet on who they think will win. The grand total profit is split between all of the businesses. So that's why everyone tries to participate. If you don't participate you don't get a part of the cut. The grand winners—two small business owners—also get a plaque to display on their business for the year. It's a whole thought-out event. It lasts the whole month, competitions commencing every Saturday.

"Quiet down everyone. It's time to draw teams." She reaches into the wooden barrel and starts pulling names. Annie and Bobbie are on the stage now assisting with the name drawing. Constance adjusts her reading glasses on her nose and reads the first few couplings into the microphone. "Mason and Chloe, you are the first team." She pauses between each name while she is handed another slip from Annie. "Bobbie and Paula." She adds an extra pause for dramatic suspense. "Annie—and Olive." You are now paired together."

I hear Olive grunt from the dance floor. I try to stifle a laugh but fail miserably. The pair ended up together last year too, and they argued the whole time. Not that they don't get along. They're both self-assured. It was hilarious to watch.

"Violet and—" *Drumroll. Please be someone I get along with. Please. Please. Please!*

"—Dustin," she says, smiling in my direction.
Who's Dustin?

"Wait, are you Violet?" Grumpy says, a line appears between his brows.

I nod in reply. He lets out a long audible sigh of frustration.

My eyes widen in horror.

"I'm guessing your name is Dustin then?" I ask, although I already have a strong suspicion. He scruffs his hair and stares at me with those enticing blue eyes that I could let myself be lost in. I don't want to fall into them, but a part of me does at the same time. It's a conflicting battle.

His head sags in defeat and he nods.

"You've got to be kidding me!" I yell in protest.

The whole bar quiets to hushed whispers. They stare at us in question. Constance speaks into her microphone, "Shhh, you two. Meet me after if you have questions."

She continues to call names, but I don't hear anything. I am boiling. I set my head on the counter on top of my crossed arms. Time passes by and after a while a tap on my shoulder breaks me from my reverie. I look up and see Olive grinning at me. The bar has since thinned out and most people are gone.

"So, I can tell we both got the short end of the straw this year. At least your partner's attractive," she says.

I scoff. Spotting Dustin making his way to Constance, I follow quickly. "Wait for me!" I call over my shoulder to Olive as she shrugs and leans back against the bar.

I make it to them as they start to talk. Huffing and puffing from running to the stage, I try to catch my breath.

"Why am I in the drawing? I'm not a business owner," his deep guttural voice rumbles.

"Well, honey you are now. You took over the farm from your grandparents yesterday. Did you not?" Constance flips through a clipboard absentmindedly, seeming the least bit concerned over Dustin's reaction.

"Ummm, yes. I guess I did."

"Then, there's your answer hun. You are now a business owner and if you want to split a part of the profit, you need to participate. Don't forget to start practicing. Starting Saturday, the first event is the chicken race. Good luck."

And with that she makes eye contact with me and winks. Her short gray hair spins and is gone as fast as she made it here.

What was that wink about? I wonder.

"See you Saturday, Grumpy." I tap him on the arm and walk away.

Olive meets me at the door. "I can't stand him," I say as we leave.

"You *obviously* like him, but believe what you want!" She chuckles.

Absolutely not.

If we are stuck together, I am not going down without a fight. We might be partners, but I'm not making this easy on him.

Chapter 5

VIOLET

"**K**nock. Knock. Package incoming!"

I scurry to the front of the shop sporting a huge grin. "Laura! You are a lifesaver! I was so worried it wouldn't come today."

"You know it, I never disappoint. You were my last stop for the day."

"Thank you! Thank you!" I gush as I grab the package she places in my arms.

"No problem, Violet. I hope you enjoy the rest of your day!"

"You too!"

I eagerly tear open the box, finding my new laptop safely cushioned inside. It's nothing special, but definitely better than the tower in my office that's never been replaced. I rush with the laptop to my office to set it up. I unplug everything and set it all in a large cardboard box in the corner of the room. I will have to save everything and transfer it later. I can't wait to have one that is more reliable and that will load faster than a snail's pace.

I lift the large tower and scoot it across the wooden desk. As it inches closer to the edge, a purple notebook slides underneath onto the soft carpet. I pick up the journal and brush off the surface, smoothing it with the back of my palm to reveal a bouquet on the cover filled with baby's breath, lavender, and violets. I've seen this before. A memory from my teen years flashes in my mind.

"What are you writing about, Ms. Burton?" I ask, curiosity lining my voice.

"Oh my sweet Violet. Sometimes when my thoughts are spinning, I scribble them down in this notebook."

"What are you thinking about?"

"Right now, I'm thinking that we should go upstairs and work on making some dinner. How does that sound?"

"Count me in!" My stomach grumbles at the mere thought. She pulls her reading glasses off and shuts the notebook, sliding it into the bottom drawer and locking it.

Ms. Burton is like the grandmother I never had. She's living in the cozy cottage retirement home now on the other side of the street. She was always so secretive about this notebook of hers. I can't believe it's been here after all of this time. And now it's in my hands. I can't help but feel like I'm betraying her trust by opening it, but I'm itching to read her words and I can't wait until I see her tomorrow. I need to know what she was writing about. Hesitantly, I open the first page. Her signature scent of rose and patchouli escape the pages.

I gasp at what I find written.

Dear H,

Today exceeded all of my expectations. The Not So Secret Garden was bustling with customers. Flower orders were flying in left and right with it being graduation and wedding season. I couldn't keep up with all of the business. I never needed to hire employees before; the stream of customers had been steady, but it wasn't something I couldn't handle on my own. Then I saw my best friend's face heading around the line out of the door. Lily. Her brown hair flowed down her shoulders. Her daughter, Violet, was at her side. She looked just like a younger replica of her mother. The pair jogged to the front of the line and asked if I needed any help taking orders. Of course, I agreed willingly. I was thankful for the love my friend had for me and my passions. The line soon dwindled to a few customers, and I was so grateful for the help. They made it all the more clear that I needed to hire some form of summer help. That's when the idea struck me. Violet had turned fifteen and had just received a work permit. Lily had been talking about it a few days earlier confessing to me how fast Violet had been growing up. And this was so true. One minute she was a baby barely uttering more than a word when I'd babysit for Lily and John. Now she's becoming a woman. If she's up for the job, she would be the perfect fit.

When I offered her a part-time job, Violet agreed with eagerness, wanting to learn all there was about flowers and running a business. I could see that same sparkle in her eyes that I too have had for years. Hopefully this will be the start to a wonderful summer, where I may be able to get a break too. Everything is lining up perfectly. If she has a love for the shop as much as I do, maybe one day it could be hers, to continue my legacy.

I wish I could find the courage to send you these letters I write for you. Telling you all about my life, and then maybe I'd get a letter back from you and hear about yours. But that thought is silly. There's no way you'd feel the same way I do. So these will continue to stay hidden in this notebook for eternity.

With Love,
Darcy Burton

A couple of tears trickle down my face as I read the words scrawled in cursive across the page. In fact, her signature purple fountain pen still sits upon her desk when I visit. It's so interesting to see the events that I experienced through her eyes. To hear about my mother was more gut wrenching. How could I forget my first day on the job and all the joy I felt to be a part of something?

I flip through the pages, finding hundreds of entries. Each dated and signed alike. It will be interesting to read all of them, but my guilt eats away at me. How would she feel about me reading these letters? And who is H, her secret love, maybe? I am most definitely getting all of the details when I visit.

Chapter 6

DUSTIN

"**Y**ou did this on purpose," I say.

"I did no such thing." My grandpa chuckles while starting up the side-by-side. We use this as the main transportation around the farm to haul tools. He drives us to the edge of the fence that needs repairing. A large section was hit by some trees that fell during a wind storm just before I arrived. The wire needed to be clipped and re-connected in a couple of huge parts using splicers. We also had to fix the tensioning and replace a few wooden posts.

"You knew the events started Monday. You called to make me come back so that I would be stuck participating," I grumble.

"Dustin, my poor grandson. Who is in perfect shape. Young and full of life. Did you expect your grandmother and I to participate in the events? I didn't make you do anything. Last year we barely made it out unscathed. Some of the days involved sports. I strained my hip and was in the hospital for a few days."

"I didn't know that. Why didn't you tell me?" I say, concern etching my voice.

"Because you've been gone. I didn't think it was that big of a deal. It was only a minor strain. I'm fine."

"Well, it is a big deal to me. I would have come and helped if I'd known."

"It's in the past now and not worth arguing over. You're here now." *Seems like someone had a change of heart.* We pass some cows grazing on the freshly sprouted grass. "You're probably wondering why we even participate. But it truly does help with raising funds for the farm. It's a good business investment."

"Don't worry, I'm not going to try to get out of it. I know how much it helps you out. I'll put in an effort even though my partner and I don't get along."

"Violet and you don't get along?"

"How do you—"

He cuts me off, "Constance called. Brought me up to speed. And for the record, Violet is a pretty, kind, and motivated young woman. She's been through a lot in her life. Take it easy on her. Besides, you two would make a fine couple."

That one does it. I tilt my head back and laugh so hard my stomach aches. There is no way. We can't even stand each other.

"What has she been through?" I'm almost positive the whole town knows and this is why he said something.

"That's for her to tell you and for me to keep my mouth shut about. Just know she hasn't had things easy. So be good to her."

This peaks my interest even more, but I don't have to dwell. The farmhouse comes into view. The inviting wrap around porch circles the front. The home is modestly sized with white aluminum siding. Hanging plants swing slightly, filled with colorful pansies. The slight breeze strikes the wind chimes. They sing a song that brings back memories of my childhood.

It feels like I am finally home.

Farther in the field off to the side of the farmhouse is where I'm staying for the foreseeable future. The small A-frame house matches the farmhouse's colors perfectly. My grandpa and I built it years ago. We cut the wood using the sawmill. Built with blood, sweat, and tears. So many nails pounded into it, hours spent creating a unique home. I wasn't sure why he wanted us to build it together when I was young. They had room in the farmhouse. Although now it becomes clear. He wanted me here all along.

The side-by-side comes to a stop in front of the house.

My grandmother calls out the front door, "Lunch is ready, boys!"

I hurry knowing she makes the best sandwiches. I feel almost like a kid again, even though I'm thirty and far from it.

"What are you doing here?" Violet asks, crossing her arms. A scowl sits on her face.

I will admit, my grandpa was right, she is pretty—who am I kidding, she's beautiful. Her long hair is up in a ponytail, but strands fall from her face on both sides, framing it in a perfect messy way. Her hazel eyes stare through me. Almost as if she can decode all of my thoughts.

But I despise her. *Keep telling yourself that.*

"Umm hello? What are you doing here?" She waves her hands in front of my face.

"Oh—" I clear my throat. "I'm here so we can practice for the chicken race."

"Seriously? You want to practice with me?" She gasps, putting her hand on her forehead, pretending to faint.

"Yes, do you have time now? Don't take this the wrong way, but I don't want you to slow us down tomorrow."

"Ha! There he is. I'm glad you're back, Grumpy. If anyone is going to slow us down, it's you." Her pointer finger stabs my chest.

"Ouch." I rub where her finger just made contact.

"Don't be dramatic. Come on, let's go, no one's here now anyway I can close up early for the day."

"I'll wait for you outside *fuddy-duddy.*" I use the nickname I gave her yesterday, knowing all too well it agitates her. The glare she sends my way confirms it.

Chapter 7

VIOLET

"**W**hat do you mean we can't just use any chicken?" Dustin scratches his head, looking perplexed.

"Everyone is assigned a chicken at random. Ours is Helga. And we already have the biggest disadvantage out of all the teams."

"What do you mean by that?"

"She's the largest chicken weighing in at eight point five pounds. A Golden Buff Orpington."

"How do you know all of that, are you a chicken whisperer or something? And how do you know its weight?"

"There's a chart, of course."

"Of course!" he mocks me.

"It's all in the email."

"What email?"

"The one Constance sent us with the details we need for tomorrow's competition."

"What are you talking about?"

Is he kidding me?

I huff, "This is going to be a rough week and we're definitely a *fowl* match." Dustin stares at me, dumbfounded. The joke must have flown way over his head. "Get it! Fowl—match. Chickens are considered fowl. It has a ring to it."

"I got it, it just wasn't funny." He shrugs, and I give him the side-eye.

It's just four weeks, I tell myself. *You can do this.* After this month we can go back to being strangers. We can act like we never even met in the first place. It will all go back to normal, and I can go back to my daily routines that don't involve anyone else. Like that certain *someone* who is partnered with me right now. I can't seem to escape his presence.

Walking up and down the sidewalk we look for the chicken, with no luck whatsoever. After some time, Dustin breaks the silence. "Since we are partners and need to work together for the challenges' sake, it'd be nice to know some more about you other than the fact that you own The Not So Secret Garden."

"What do you want to know?"

"What's your favorite movie and why? What's your favorite food? What's your middle name?"

"Those are super random things." I continue walking along the sidewalk. "And I don't think anyone has ever asked me what my middle name was before." I look behind a trash can only to find an adorable Silkie. I pet her on the head and continue my search. "*Shrek* is my favorite movie. When I'm sad it makes me forget about all my worries. The noise in my head dies down. My insecurities, doubts, and frustrations fade away. It never fails to put a smile on my face no matter how bad the day was."

I didn't mean to get so deep with him. But maybe it's good that we get to know each other. We're partners; we have to work together as a team. Teammates normally need to get along. "What was the next question again?"

"Favorite food."

"Oh! That's right. My favorite food is a tiebreaker between macaroni and cheese or pepperoni rolls. Don't get me started on how amazing the pepperoni rolls from The String Cheese are. Joe can make any other meal dull in comparison. Its carb filled with cheesy, doughy, greasy pepperoni goodness. It's what dreams are made of." There's no doubt about what I'm having for dinner tonight.

"And my middle name is Tarynn."

"Interesting."

Interesting. That's all he has to say? After I just spilled everything about myself. "What about you?"

"My favorite movie is *Grown Ups* because it's hilarious. Nothing can change my opinion on that. Especially when they play a game of arrow roulette. My favorite food is lasagna. And my middle name is Cole."

"Interesting." I chuckle. "Who knew you loved *Grown Ups*. I'm surprised you've seen that movie."

He sighs, "Enough talking, let's find this damn chicken already." I roll my eyes. "You were the one asking the questions."

"And you were the one who went on and on. I didn't ask for your whole life story."

I mutter curse words under my breath and stride away.

Can he be any more infuriating?

We spend the next hour searching high and low looking for Miss Helga. She is one tough egg to crack. Everywhere we look there is always a different chicken and she is nowhere to be found. I'm starting to lose hope that we will be able to find her. And I'm getting ready to call it quits and go home. Dustin isn't making this experience very pleasant anyways.

"Aha there she is! In a flowerpot!" I shout to Dustin as he jogs from Cat's & Novels to me in front of Fix-Its.

By the time he reaches me he is out of breath. Beads of sweat trickle down his forehead. And for a miniscule moment I can't help but get swept away, admiring how attractive he is. And I mean a microscopic moment, because then I remember who he is.

"That. Chicken. Is. Mine." His breathy voice strains, gasping for air. His arms stretch to reach and grab her.

"Slow—down, it kind of looks like she is about to lay an egg."

"No way, she's not. I got you Miss Helga. I won't let Violet upset you," he says way nicer than he's ever spoken to me.

"No!" Dustin shouts. Everything is in slow motion. The brown egg slowly drops out of the chicken as he lifts her into the air. And the best possible thing happens. *Well, for me at least.* The karma I manifested only yesterday. But *so* much better.

The egg flops to the ground and crunches as it falls hard onto his work boots. The shell shatters into a million pieces. Dark yellow and clear liquid sprays everywhere, painting his clothes in the sticky mess. It continues to drip down the fabric. He stands as still as a statue, holding the chicken midair. A look of pure horror is edged in the frown lines next to his lips. I try to suppress my emotions. But I can't contain an outburst of the loudest laugh that has ever left my mouth. It's ugly, boisterous, and I snort. I just about drop down on the ground and roll. This is comedy gold.

A few moments pass and he's still frozen in space holding the chicken midair. "Shit," he mutters.

"Not shit, actually yolk!" I say between bits of laughter.

Dustin's lip curls up in the corner. I think that maybe I'm imagining it. Although, I'm not, it's clear as day. One of my jokes finally landed. He can't deny that I made that grin appear. But I know he will, the man doesn't know how to laugh. I wish he'd let out a little chuckle. Because I'm starting to think I'm not as funny as I am in my head.

Helga sits in his arms looking the least bit impressed with our shenanigans.

"Let's clean you up. Hand me the chicken please." Dustin places the chicken in my arms, and I smooth my hand down her feathers. "You're safe now, the mean man won't hurt you anymore."

He rolls his eyes and grumbles, "I wasn't mean."

"Just one more trial run and then I think we're ready for the big day tomorrow." I hold Helga in my arms, waiting for the go-ahead.

"Three—two—one—go!" Dustin shouts from across the field. I place Helga on the grass. "Come on Helga, do you want some mealworms? You are beautiful! Strong! Independent! Fluffy!" He shouts a bunch of compliments at the chicken.

And you may be wondering, why is he yelling positive affirmations to a chicken, also known as Helga? Well, that may be my fault. No. It is my fault. I may have told him if he says positive affirmations and speaks encouraging phrases to Helga she'll run faster. I told him that every team does it. He believed me.

I lied.

Honestly it kind of seems like it's working. At first it was a joke. I just wanted to see how far he would take it. Now we're getting somewhere. And maybe, we have a shot at placing in the top three.

At first, I thought there wasn't much hope for even placing in the top seven.

She starts trotting along the grass, bee-lining it straight to Dustin. When she is about five feet from him, she decides to stop in place. She lifts one of her legs and stands still as stone. It's as if she can read my thoughts.

Everything we've practiced flew right out the window. Helga is ready for a nap. She had enough for the day. I don't blame her, we've been at it for hours.

"Helga, come here. Remember what we've practiced." He motions with his hands full of treats, "You can get mealworms. I'm your favorite person, come here." Helga doesn't move a muscle.

I scoff. "As if. She can tell a bad egg when she sees one."

He sizes me up, "Your jokes aren't funny."

"Gee thanks. Like I need your validation. I'm perfectly confident in my ability to make people laugh. You are the exception," I point my finger at him, "You don't have a silly bone in your body."

He shrugs and throws a handful of mealworms on the ground. "Well, me and this *body*," he stabs a finger to his chest, "are leaving."

"Good riddance," I wave aggressively.

Helga decides now is the perfect time to move. She runs to the treats and pecks them off the ground. Dustin rolls his eyes and walks across the field in large strides. Once he reaches the trail back to town I sit on the ground and pick strands of grass. I look heavenward and say a silent prayer. *Please for the love of God, let these competitions go by faster.*

Chapter 8

VIOLET

"These pop tarts are the best thing I have ever tasted in my life," Dustin says as we all continue to munch on the freshly baked strawberry pastries and sip on warm coffee.

Olive was not kidding when she said she was making strawberry pop tarts. This is the most mouthwatering pastry I have ever tasted. With golden flaky edges coated in butter, white icing drizzled on top, homemade strawberry filling bursting from the edges, I'm in heaven. These will definitely be part of my go-to breakfast stop.

"I told you not to miss trying out my new recipe! And to think, you almost said no," Olive says with a smug grin. She knows she can bake anything to perfection. And she's not afraid to prove it.

"I will never even think of denying another invitation to try anything you make. Ever again."

"Can you stop moaning and just eat it already?" Mason says.

"I'm not moaning," Dustin says.

"Yes, you are!" Olive, Mason and I say in unison.

We all laugh. "Don't make them so delicious and I won't," he says with a shrug. He shoves another bite into his mouth.

I can't blame him. They are that good.

"How is training going?" Mason asks.

"Honestly better than expected. We have the chicken race in the bag," The part I leave out is how our last trial was a disaster. Olive looks at me with a smirk, insinuating something. I ignore her taunting gaze the instant her eyes stare into mine. I know that look.

"I'll take that as a compliment," Dustin grumbles.

After everyone leaves the shop, ranting and raving over her new menu addition, Olive and I are the only ones left.

"Now that everyone's gone, I have to tell you what happened yesterday."

"What happened?" I ask, curiosity lining my voice.

"Out of all the people I expected to show up, guess who did?"

"I have no clue?" I think I know exactly who showed up.

Chad.

The infamous Chad.

Their on and off again relationship reminds me of a rollercoaster. Not some bunny hopping slow ride. More like one of those ones that makes your stomach drop to your feet as it flips upside down. He's a nice guy when he *wants* to be. But he has major commitment issues. He breaks her heart, puts on the charm and she takes him back. It's been a never-ending cycle of disappointment. She has a soft spot when it comes to him. Not that I can blame her; he is charming, just like Prince Charming, minus the sculpted face and long blonde hair. Okay, maybe I have an obsession with *Shrek*. Can you blame me?

"It was Chad!" she exclaims.

Told you.

"He had the audacity to show up with his new girlfriend. It's only been three days! Three days since we broke up. He couldn't have the decency to wait even as little as a week before he moved on."

"Oh, Olive, I'm so sorry you had to see that. I can't believe he would show up with someone else at your shop." Okay, maybe I can believe he would do that. He is that kind of jerk. I mean come on, his name is Chad. "What did you do?" I have a feeling things didn't go well by the look of pure rage shooting from her green eyes directly into my soul. I'm just glad I'm not on the receiving end this time.

"I'll get there, Vivi. I didn't even get to the best part—" She pauses, staring at her coffee while it swirls. The ice cubes race each other in a spinning whirlpool. "He showed up with Chelsea. I could have screamed. She has had it out for me since elementary school. Remember eighth grade when Will kissed me during study hall? Well she had a crush on him and the evil sprouted from that day on. She was so mad that he liked me that she made a vow to make my life miserable. I swear she is Regina George's twin. I know she still has it out for me. It's been her mission to steal every single guy I show interest in. Then what she did to you in high school. Unforgivable. Are you hearing..."

"Woah. Woah. Woah. Slow down," I say, tapping my fingers on the coffee cup. I do not need to think about what happened in the past. "I remember what she did to me. We don't have to talk about that. Back to what you did. What *did* you do?"

"Ha! Well, I was going to act civil until he came up to the counter and flaunted his new *relationship* in my face. He grabbed her hand and kissed her right at the counter. So, I did what any self-respecting person would do—I threw a cup of cold brew all over him. Then I threatened him. She got caught in the crossfires and I can't say that I regret it." A menacing grin crosses her face.

"No way Olive, you didn't!" I laugh so hard coffee shoots out of my mouth. "And what did you threaten him with?" I step around the counter to grab a rag to clean up the mess I made on the floor.

"If he ever steps foot in my coffee shop again, I wouldn't be so nice. I will use hot coffee next time. He knows I'm not bluffing. And the asshole could go to Annie's Diner for coffee or just make it himself. As long as he's out of my life for good."

I laugh so hard tears start to form in the corners of my eyes. What I would have given to see the look on his coffee covered face.

"I don't think I'll be hearing from him anytime soon. And I will admit it's time to move on from him. He dragged his feet out of the door, coffee soaked and all. Chelsea hung on his arm scowling at me as they left, stomping out of the doors. And it was worth all the mess I had to clean up."

"I am so relieved to hear you say that. I think you dodged a bullet with that one." And this is the truth.

"Come in dear. You're late. I was just about to leave to play a round of bingo, this better be good."

"Nice to see you too Darcy," I sing-song while skipping in the door.

"Oh please sit down and relax, I have all day. What's that?" She points in the direction of the paper bag I'm holding.

"Nothing! You don't have time so I'll just leave." I know all too well that she will want what's in this bag. I spin on my heel and rush out the door. I know what she's going to say. Something like, "Wait! Please!" Or maybe, "I'm so sorry. Stay all day, Violet."

"Wait!"

I told you.

"Come back, please. I'm sorry; I didn't mean it honey. What's in the bag?" Okay, maybe I wasn't exactly right, but I was pretty close.

"Only a couple strawberry pop tarts from the Olive Bean. But it's okay if you want to play bingo. I'll be going."

"No! No! Get back here, it's so nice to see you. Please stay all day, Violet dear."

There it is!

"I thought so," I mumble under my breath, smiling at our exchange. She's my only family left. I love her more than anything in the world. I also love to tease her; besides, I inherited most of my puns from her. It's been getting harder to tell when it is a good or bad day. Today seems to be going well. She seems to remember everything, not questioning or becoming confused.

She takes a huge bite of the sugary goodness and grins with delight. "You're unusually bubbly and smiling today. What's going on?" she says as she continues to devour the treat.

"Nothing much is new. I don't know what you're talking about."

"Liar! I've known you since you were a baby. I know you better than I know myself. It's a man, isn't it?"

"What? No..."

"Yes! That's it. What's his name."

"I don't know what you're talking about."

"It's Dustin, isn't it? I heard you were paired with him for this year's small business games. He's handsome, why wouldn't you be head over heels with him?"

I blush scarlet. "What? Ew! One, I'm absolutely not. And two, how do you know what he looks like?"

"I'm not dead yet. We do have phones in here. Constance keeps me updated on you anyways."

"Constance and I are going to have a chat."

"Absolutely not, she is my only form of entertainment in this place other than bingo."

"You know you don't have to stay here. I didn't want you to leave. I would have taken care of you." My voice softens.

"I wanted to be here with my friends. Besides, you need your own space to blossom."

"Like flowers in spring," I say, smiling at the memory. It's something she always told me growing up. After I lost everything.

She continues to eat as we sit in comfortable silence.

"I came here for one more thing. I have something to show you." I pull out the purple notebook from my purse and hand it over to her.

She gasps in surprise as one hand grasps the notebook, the other over her heart. "I thought this was gone forever. I couldn't find it anywhere."

"I found it under the old tower computer. The one that you've had since you opened the store. Would you mind if I read them?"

"Of course you can read them! I wrote about so many things. About the shop, about my life. Even tips on running the shop. It may be helpful to you. I don't mind."

The question lingers in the depths of my mind. I might as well come out with it. "Who is H?"

"No one important." Her answer is clipped.

That was not the answer I was expecting.

"Look who's being evasive about a man now?"

"Touché. Maybe once you tell me I'll tell you, how's that sound?"

So, she doesn't deny it was a love interest.

"Okay, I'll let you get to bingo. Knock 'em dead."

"I will! Don't fail me at that chicken race!"

"I won't. See you next week!"

I end up leaving with more questions than I came with. Who is H and why did she look so sad when I handed her the notebook? I might have to do some investigation work on my own.

Chapter 9

VIOLET

"It gives me great pleasure to welcome you all to day one of Thornwood Valley's Annual Spring Festivities. Today's event is the chicken race!" Constance announces to the town with a megaphone. "I know everyone hates it when I talk about rules, but listen carefully. We've had issues in previous years when the rules were not addressed. So, I have to read them now."

A few people boo the idea of rules. Constance rolls her eyes. "Hey! No booing!" She scruffs her head and continues on with her spiel. "Rule number one, don't nudge or push the chickens to help them. Rule number two, don't move from your spot on the line. Rule number three, no profanities; there are children in attendance. Please. When you hear the whistle the partner at the red line will release your chicken. The first chicken to make it past the green line will win this challenge. Once each team passes the finish line we will keep track of your placing. The top seven teams will be put on the bulletin board to proceed to next week's competition. And the last two teams to cross will be eliminated. For anyone watching there are refreshments on the tables to my right." She points a manicured nail in the direction of the drinks.

All of the teams are lined up in a straight line on the grass field. Olive stands next to me, wearing a green sweatshirt. Every team has color coordinating shirts with our names on the back. Dustin and I both wear purple sweatshirts. Our faces are painted with a purple stripe under each of our eyes. And I'm wearing a matching sweat band around my forehead. Dustin refused to wear one, but I don't blame him. We all look the part, but we also look absolutely ridiculous. I think the gossip mill purposely gave our teams colors based on Olive and I's names. I wouldn't be surprised.

Constance's voice echoes through the megaphone again. "Contestants please make sure you are standing on the painted line in the grass. Get ready to release your chicken in three—two—one." The whistle sounds in a flash.

I release Helga to the wolves. She must have stage fright or something because she just stands there, unmoving. *Do not look at the other teams and focus only on our team, Violet.* It's extremely hard not to peek at the competition to see if they are having any luck. Dustin is straight across from me shaking the bag of mealworms, looking laser focused. "Helga, you can do this. You are stunning! Glowing! Radiating the essence of love!" *What in the world is he saying?* "Don't give up on me now, remember what we practiced! You are strong! You lay the largest and best eggs out of all the hens!" he shouts over the roaring noises surrounding us.

She eats up his encouraging words and starts trudging through the grass straight to Dustin. I'm screaming, throwing my hands up in the air. Hoping that she will continue strutting to make us win this one. It would be the first time an Orpington ever won the week one competition.

Tourists and locals surround the park, their muffled voices cheering for different teams. I feel the adrenaline pouring from the atmosphere. Some even shout, "go Helga." I feel like a proud chicken mother. Helga's at the final stretch of grass before the green line. She only has three feet until she passes the finish line.

Come on Helga, you can do this.

Out of the corner of my eye I see Mason's Americana two feet away. She's so close my hands tremble. Sweat drips down my back, riveting across my cool skin. I've always lost the chicken race, and I swear if we could just get this one win, I might cry, happy tears, of course.

Then Helga does it, she speeds up with every ounce of energy left and races across the finish line, earning our team first place. I can't believe it! Dustin scoops her up, jumping up and down and spinning her around.

Constance's voice booms through the megaphone. "We have a winner! Helga from team purple, they are now the champions of the chicken race!"

The crowd of fifty or so tourists and townsfolk roars. Then the next few chickens cross the finish line and are announced one by one until all of the teams cross. I don't hear any of it though, I'm too focused on the buzz of our win. My face is beaming with a huge genuine smile. As soon as I hear, "That concludes this week's chicken race. Great work everyone!" from Constance, I beeline it across the track straight to Dustin. He pulls me and Helga into a bone crushing embrace. Smiling with joy, he spins us around through the air. My feet dangle off the ground, my hair swooshes around my face. Dustin sets me down back on solid ground. We stare at each other for a few minutes, grinning in triumph. For a split second—which feels like forever—our eyes lock and I get this tingly spark of emotion in my chest. Or it's just the nerves combined with dizziness from the spin. I fall into his blue-eyed spell and can't break our eye contact.

I can't believe he smiled.

Constance's voice brings me back to reality. "I have one more announcement before we get to the food. Annie's is providing ribs, chicken, and fries for everyone. This year is special because it marks the twentieth anniversary. So with that being said, with each challenge there will be a small prize. Team purple, you won an all-expenses paid dinner at The String Cheese tonight only. So, you better take advantage of it!" She looks in my direction. "Also, the second and third place winners will get a free pepperoni roll coupon!"

This has to be a ploy; she knows very well Dustin and I didn't get along. Bigger forces are at play here. Why does it have to be tonight only? The matchmaking forces of the gossip mill are definitely behind this. But I can't complain. I am a sucker for that cheese filled pepperoni roll. And I will be eating dinner there with or without Dustin.

"Oh, I almost forgot! The winning team can only get their free meal if they both show up." Constance's voice booms yet again. The woman can read my mind; it's infuriating and kind of concerning.

"You sure looked chummy with Dustin." Olive pokes my side.

"Oh please, we were just celebrating a win. Nothing's going on."

"Mhmm, keep telling yourself that. I saw the way you were looking at each other." Then she skips away to grab some food.

We were just celebrating a win. That's all.

Chapter 10

DUSTIN

The thrill of winning the chicken race hasn't dulled. You'd think I'm a celebrity by the way the townies are treating me. Every person that passes along the sidewalk stops to tell me, *congratulations,* or they ask, *how did you ever think to tell Helga positive affirmations? That was genius.* I answer with a quick, *I've done a lot of research into poultry and how they interact with humans.* It's a bullshit reply I came up with; I have no clue why it worked. Violet told me everyone did it. I was naive to trust her. If we didn't win, I would've looked like a fool. But we did, so there's no need to dwell on it now.

My phone dings with an incoming text from my best friend, Nolan.

NOLAN

Farmer Dusty. How's it going?

DUSTIN

Great.

NOLAN

Are you missing your apartment yet?

DUSTIN

Not at all.

NOLAN

Good, because you're not getting it back.

My phone begins ringing in my hand. I pick up on the third chime.

"Hey." He murmurs through the line.

"I didn't feel like texting. It takes up too much time."

"I get that." I say. Nolan was never one to spend much time thinking about anything other than work.

"I've been trying to get ahold of you, but it kept saying message not delivered."

"We don't have good service on the farm."

"That's unfortunate. Why don't you hook up a booster or something."

"Don't get me started on that subject."

"Okay, okay. I won't piss you off. I called to tell you that you are so lucky I could take over your apartment's lease. But I guess I'm lucky too. It's nice being closer to the best restaurants."

Is it crazy that I don't miss it? The thought comes and goes from my mind.

"Believe me. You're a lifesaver."

"Well, I got to get back to work. Keep me updated, *Farmer Dusty*. Don't come crawling back to your apartment in a few months, it's mine now."

"What an asshole," I grumble.

"I heard that!" he yells and then I quickly press the end call button. I pocket my phone and continue down the sidewalk.

I stop when I reach The String Cheese. I pull out a rod iron chair and sit, waiting for Violet to show up.

The winning team can only get their free meal if they both show up. I want to wipe the sound of Constance's voice from the confines of my mind. That woman is always up to something. First, declaring me a small business owner after one day. Now, she's scheming with Violet and I. I've gotta watch what I say around her.

Violet comes walking down the sidewalk with Olive at her side, still wearing her competitive getup. She tilts her head back and laughs at something Olive says. Her hair is frazzled and pulled back with a purple band. Her nose crinkles and her cheeks redden around the purple lines painted across her face.

She's always laughing, it makes me wonder why. Is she *really* always that happy? It infuriates me. But also intrigues me.

I can't stand her one bit. And yet I feel myself pulled to her every movement.

After our miraculous, close call of a win, when I pulled her into my arms and swung her and Helga in a circle—there was a moment when I forgot we didn't get along. It was a flicker of a few seconds. Short and fleeting. Her presence is captivating. I'll admit it.

Her smile falters when she sees me waiting for her. But I can't quite read the expression that spreads over her face. Is it loathing? Or something else? I don't have time to think because she stands in front of me and says, "let's go, I'm in desperate need of something to eat." I shrug and follow her into the shop.

Chapter 11

VIOLET

"Constance really loves using a megaphone. A little too much. It's more like an obsession," Dustin says while we wait in line at The String Cheese.

"Yeah, she gets a kick out of it every year. I swear she tunes it up and keeps it on a pedestal."

"I can picture it completely dust free all year, sparkling with a spotlight shining over it." He looks at the menu and then back at me. "So, what's good here? I've never been."

"What did you just say? You've never been here! I thought you visited your grandparents' farm every summer."

"I came every summer until I turned eighteen. My grandmother always made home-cooked meals. And at their house I wasn't allowed to deny her cooking. So, we never ate out, not even once.

Her cooking is superior to anything I have ever tasted, so I can't complain. She makes a delicious apple crumble pie."

"I love apple pie." I'm a foodie through and through. I'll try anything that sounds good. I fit in a run or two each week to burn off all of the excess calories, but I'm not obsessed with it. I love my curves and I'm not afraid to eat.

"She made one fresh today. I can save you a slice. While we prepare for the next challenge."

"Why are you being so nice to me all of a sudden?" The thought bursts out of my mouth before I have time to think.

Something I do more often than not.

I shouldn't question it, because I can't resist apple pie.

"I'm starting to realize you're not as bad as I thought. Don't let it get to your head."

"Does that mean we are friends?" I gasp, covering my mouth with one hand.

"Not even close, merely forced acquaintances."

"What can I get for the big winners? Choose any meal and drink." Joe, also known as Pizza Joe, says with a big grin.

"Do you like pepperoni and cheese?" I whisper to Dustin.

"Who doesn't?" he whispers back. His breath against my ear makes me tremble. I can't tell if that's a good or bad thing.

I roll my eyes. "Can we get a mega pepperoni roll with extra marinara? Also, a root beer for me please. What do you want to drink?" I turn towards Dustin.

"I'll have the same as you."

"Anything for the winners," Joe says scribbling down our order on a guest check pad. "Daisy will be out with your food and drinks when they are ready."

"Thanks Joe."

We chose a table in the center of the dining room. There are a few other tables filled with locals grabbing dinner. "I don't mean to be nosy, but do you ever drink?" Dustin asks sincerely.

I freeze. I wasn't expecting that question. And I am most definitely not ready to divulge that information.

"I'm drinking a root beer." I try to evade his question.

"You know what I mean," he says while resting his arm on the table.

I'm hopelessly trying to come up with something to change the topic.

A few moments of silence pass and I am panicking. My skin is itchy all over, my palms are sweating, and I feel like I'm going to pass out from the anxiety.

"Wait, what is the next challenge?" he asks while Daisy sets our drinks on the table. I smile shakily at her, and she smiles back.

I'm grateful for the change in subject. I can tell by his furrowed brows and facial expressions that he doesn't want to push me. Something about the way he changed the subject and trusted that I wasn't ready to talk about it made my walls unfreeze a tiny bit.

Do I trust him? I don't know yet. It's too soon to tell. And definitely too soon to release the floodgates holding back my deepest secrets.

"Here's your food, let me know if I can get you anything else. And congrats, that was one heck of a win!"

"Thanks Daisy, that means a lot," I say.

Dustin shoves a huge slice of the cheesy dough in his mouth and moans.

"This is the best pepperoni roll I've ever had in my life. No wonder it's your favorite food," he mumbles, still chewing.

"See I told you, nothing beats it." I laugh while taking another bite. Not even caring about the grease all over my face. Something about him is starting to make me feel at ease. I don't have to pretend to be anything but myself around him. My thoughts are so conflicting, one minute I feel at ease, the next I can't stand him. "The next challenge is to solve a 1,000-piece puzzle. We are each given the same puzzle. They pick a new one every year to keep it fair."

He chews and then looks concerned. "I'm horrible at puzzles, what about you?"

"I am the worst. So we better spend some time practicing."

"Lunch. Wednesday. It's a date." He holds out his hand for me to shake.

My brows quirk up and my eyes widen. It's at this moment when his blue eyes widen as well, realizing his slip up. I shrug it off and say, "It's a strictly strategizing, acquaintance date." And I shake his hand. The touch sends a warm zap through my fingers, and I pull away quickly.

Did he feel that too? This month is going to test me.

Chapter 12

DUSTIN

"Woah, did you need to bring that many puzzles?"

"Shut up and help me!" Violet's muffled shout is blocked by the leaning tower of puzzles in her arms. There are at least eight of them stacked on top of each other. I swear she's always carrying stacks of things that are way too hard for one person to balance. At least this time I'm here to help, because we don't need another incident to happen.

"Sheesh you're the grouchy one today." I grab four puzzles off the mountain, and I finally see her face. Violet's hair flows across her eyes, pieces of hair that came loose from the messy bun all contained in a large clip on the back of her head. I reach out and swipe a strand, tucking it behind her ear so she can see.

And that's the only reason I'm finding an excuse to touch her.

I set the stack I grabbed on the kitchen table. Then I grab the remaining ones from her and set them on top. She stands there still, mouth agape. Her hazel eyes glisten with curiosity while she surveys the interior of my A-frame house.

"This place is—breathtaking."

She spins around, taking in the open concept. Hardwood floors and wood beaded ceilings. A dark butcher block counter adorns the wall with a fridge and stove. Stairs lead to the open loft with a queen bed. Everything is in neutral shades. I knew she would love this place. After seeing the inside of the flower shop, I can tell she appreciates woodwork.

"My grandfather and I built this place together during a few summers when I stayed. This was always my favorite place to escape everything when I was young."

"I can see why; it's quaint and cozy." She does another spin, taking in everything. "And warm and inviting."

"So, did you buy every puzzle?"

"I had a feeling they would get the puzzle from Cat's & Novel's. So, I bought every one in stock." She shrugs like it was no big deal.

"You do know by participating we get the same benefits as every other team. So we technically don't even have to win any of the challenges." I thought about this last night and realized we are trying so hard to win, but for what? We don't really have to put in any extra time. We could skate by and lose this next challenge so that we don't have to take part in any more.

"First off, Constance said there will be prizes for the winners because of the anniversary. Second off, I want that plaque for the front of my shop." Her eyes squint and she crosses her arms. I think I hit a nerve.

"What's so great about a plaque?"

"Whaaaaa—everything! Just by displaying that on the front of your business you get more customers. Plus, bragging rights for the year. Not that I care to brag, but I've lost every single one I've entered. Chelsea has won the past two years. It's time someone beats her."

"Got it. I will train at all hours so that we can get first place."

"I'll believe it when I see it. Now, let's quit wasting time," she says while sitting down on a chair and scooting closer to the table.

We started out with a puzzle that had a red barn surrounded by a field of sunflowers three hours ago. All that we have to prove for it are a measly four sunflowers, the roof of the barn, and a half-eaten apple pie. My head is throbbing from the amount of sugar and mental activity. Whoever said a puzzle was easy, was lying.

"What happened with Chelsea?"

"What makes you think something happened?" She looks down at the pieces, avoiding eye contact.

"I could tell by the determination on your face when you said someone had to beat her this year."

"Well, I guess it's public news around here since everyone knows everything so I might as well come out with it. Jackson and I dated for about two years when I was in high school. Long story short, I went to surprise him on his birthday at his place after we graduated and I found him and Chelsea together. Turns out he was cheating on me with her for months. I was so clueless."

"I'm so sorry that happened to you."

"It's okay, it was a long time ago, but that's why I have a hard time trusting anyone."

"Don't worry; we will beat her in this competition. That's a promise."

"Thank you—Jackson also works at the post office now, so that's why I have a hard time mailing anything," she confesses, looking down at the puzzle again.

"If you ever need me to mail something for you, I'm your guy." And I mean it. I can't imagine having to face your ex in such a small town with only one option for miles.

"That means a lot." She fiddles with the pieces looking teary eyed. A few minutes pass while we concentrate on finding pieces and group them together.

"Tell me about your life in New York. Was it everything people say it is and more?" she asks while digging a fork into a half-eaten slice of pie.

"To be honest it had its moments. I really did enjoy living there. The buzz of the city. People everywhere. You could blend into a crowd of thousands of people. The thing is, I never felt more...alone." Shit, did I confess that? I've never told anyone that before. I think this puzzle is wreaking havoc with my sanity.

I've been thinking about things this past week. I still don't know whether I should stay here or move back to the city. I'm at a crossroads. Both decisions have drawbacks and advantages. It's nice to be surrounded by my family here. Work on the farm has been a refreshing change in pace. I don't miss sitting at a desk all day. But I worked so hard to build my career. I think a few more weeks will help me weigh on the decision. Will I get sick of the farming life? Is it all too fresh now?

I'm not sure.

"Living in a small town my whole life, it's felt like I could never blend in. Everyone knows everyone. So here and there I crave blending in and hiding in a crowd." She twirls her empty fork between her fingers. "Feeling alone, that's something I've spent far too long living."

I wonder what she means by that. This conversation is getting heavy. I don't think I'm ready to dive deeper. It doesn't seem like she is ready either. Though I can't help but feel a connection to her.

We're two people who've always felt lonely. Alone in a world full of people.

Chapter 13

VIOLET

It's midday and I'm sulking in my thoughts draped in a crocheted blanket Olive made for me. Snuggling against my orange and white tabby cat, Fiona, who's sprawled on the couch against my legs. I stare at the blank television screen hanging on the wall. I have so many things to do. I should be eating lunch. Or working on flower arrangements. I need to be doing something productive.

The thing is, I never felt more—alone.

Dustin's words have been replaying in my mind for the past few days. Eating away at the trauma I've been suppressing for years. I work nonstop, never allowing myself a break to sit and wallow. But our conversation has put a crack in my armor. And today I couldn't keep moving any longer.

A memory flashes through my mind from when I was fifteen.

"Violet, honey, we are going to be late if you don't hurry."

"Ten more minutes Mom!" I shout from my room.

After straightening my hair for another thirty minutes I finally jog down the stairs and hop into the back seat of our minivan.

"I'm glad you decided that we could leave," my dad says while looking back at me, a smile forming on his face from the driver's seat. He shakes his head, and his arm drapes around the back of my mom's seat while reversing out of our driveway. He always did that. It was a way to show her how much he cared for her. I don't think he even realized he did it, it was done out of habit. But it was such a small gesture that I picked up on. The love he felt for her was incomparable.

"Sorry Dad, I didn't mean to take so long," I say while flipping through songs on my iPod, popping two earbuds in.

Hours later the sky is dark, and I drift in and out of consciousness. We're almost halfway to the beach as we sit at a stoplight. When the light turns green, we continue on our way. Out of nowhere, a flash of red from the left side window shoots straight towards our car. The hatchback T-bones our minivan in seconds, sending us flipping in the air. Everything happens so fast I don't have time to process it as my vision goes black.

This is why I don't let myself think about the past. The thoughts make me queasy. I unwrap myself from the throw blanket and pat Fiona on her head. My body trembles while I smooth my hand across her fur. I rush down the stairs and stumble into the greenhouse.

Hours later I emerge from watering plants, starting new seeds, and I feel slightly better. Not much, but enough to emerge from hiding. The sky is a bright blue with wispy clouds, and I ache for a cup of warm coffee to ease my racing mind.

Grateful that Olive stays open until three every day, I walk over to grab some. When I open the door, I see Olive behind the counter spinning on a stool in circles waiting for her next customer. It puts a smile on my face. She never fails to make me laugh.

"Hi sunshine, it's a beautiful day outside!" She waves to me from the counter with a chipper demeanor. It's normally contagious, but today I'm not feeling myself.

"Coffee," I blurt, struggling to form words.

"Ha! Did you wake up on the wrong side of the bed today? What happened to, 'Hi, how are you bestie?' Or, 'It is a beautiful day, it's so nice to see you pal!'" Olive flies out of the chair and pours some coffee into a ceramic mug. Then slides it across the counter to me.

"Something like that. Sorry." I take a big gulp and scrunch my face from the strong and bitter flavor. "Thanks, I needed that. It's a black coffee kind of day. This is my third cup."

"I could tell it was a strong coffee kind of day." She shrugs and starts wiping the counter off. "So, how are you and Dustin getting along?"

"We're tolerating each other," I say while sipping slowly. "How about Annie and you?"

"Don't change the subject, you already know that Annie and I don't make the best team." She sits back down and crosses one leg over the other. "You two really seem to make a good pair. And would make an even better couple. He's good looking, you can't deny it. Especially since he's starting to grow some stubble. He's got the whole farmer appeal really setting in now." She raises her eyebrows up and down suggestively.

"Nope, definitely not. I'm not going to deny I find him attractive, but who says he would even want to date me anyway." I sigh while draining the rest of the cup down my throat.

I walk to the back of the shop to the sinks. And start scrubbing my mug with a sponge.

"You don't have to wash your cup, you know that right? There are people I hire to do that. Just kidding, you know I do all of the dishes, but seriously, I can wash your cup."

"I know, I thought I would help you out a little bit. You're always helping me." I transfer the cup to the drying section and grab an empty coffee pot to scrub.

"Violet. Look at me." I continue to scrub dishes. Avoiding her gaze. "Please look at me." I slowly drop the scouring sponge and turn to face her. "Any guy would be lucky to be with you. You are the strongest person I know. You are also extremely kind, selfless, and hardworking. Everything you survived is what made you all of those things. If he can't see that, then he's foolish. And it isn't meant to be."

"You're going to make me cry," I say while I turn to transfer the now clean pot to another sink. I dunk it into the sanitizing sink. I can't bear to look at her. I know it will open the floodgates once again.

"I'm not telling you what I think. It's what I know. And that's all that matters. I'm here for you. We're sisters by force."

"Yes, we are." I smile while finishing the last few dishes. I am so grateful that I have Olive in my corner. We may not be sisters by blood, but our bond is much stronger. And I don't know what I would do without her by my side.

Chapter 14

VIOLET

This Saturday the events are being held in Annie's Diner. It was the biggest place that had enough tables to house all of the teams. Each one is covered with white tablecloths. The mystery puzzle is wrapped in each team's color at the center of every one. Ours is covered in purple paper. Matching our sweatshirts. Now it's a waiting game until everyone arrives. Constance hasn't made an appearance yet.

Today isn't a good day for me and I'm not in the right headspace to focus. I think Dustin can tell I'm distant because his lips are turning down into a frown while looking at me. Or maybe I have some food on my teeth from the sandwich I scarfed down right before we arrived.

"Is there something on my face, or on my teeth?" I rub my face and then wipe my teeth with my tongue.

"What? No. Why?" Dustin grumbles.

Someone's testy today.

"Because you're scowling at me." I say while tapping my fingers on the table.

"You never showed up to practice for the rest of the week," he says, setting his elbow on the table and pressing his chin into his palm.

"I was busy this week. Sorry I didn't show." *Lies. I was busy, but with my emotions.*

He just stares at me, eyebrows shooting upward. Definitely not buying what I said.

"The way you're looking at me is unsettling," I say while inching my fingers closer to the puzzle.

"Good, that was my intention."

Then a loud voice booms over the speakers set up around the room. "It's time for the second competition. Before I start with the rules, please do not touch the puzzle on your table until I tell you to start."

I inch my fingers away from the puzzle and place my hand on my lap.

"Looks like someone upgraded to a microphone," he whispers, leaning in.

My lips curl into a smile. Then I get a whiff of his scent. Pine and evergreen fill my senses. It's reminiscent of walking among the tall trees in a forest. It's invigorating but not overpowering. It lingers for a moment and dissipates as he leans back.

"Everyone please, listen carefully." I jump in my seat when Constance's voice gets louder. The microphone is really working, someone should turn it down a touch. "It's time for your favorite part, the rules. Rule number one, do not use any phones to help you at all. No exceptions. Rule number two, keep your hands off the table until I say go. Rule number three, absolutely no outside help from anyone. I'm looking at you all." She points at the tourists and people from the town grouping around the sides. "And there are six of us going around keeping an eye to make sure everyone is following the rules. We are all wearing white shirts. Once you are finished, raise your hands and we will come to your table and check to make sure it is finished. We will announce the winners as we find out. The top five will move on to next week's challenge."

Dustin cracks his fingers and does a quick stretch, putting on a show. Then he takes a sip of his water. We were all given a couple of bottles of water, because this event normally takes three hours.

"Okay, get ready to start your puzzles. In three—two—one. Go!" Constance announces.

Dustin doesn't waste any time as he rips open the purple paper from the puzzle. It flies in the air, and he throws it haphazardly behind him.

"Hey! Sabotage!" Jane shouts.

Dustin pays no mind to her and continues to dump the pieces on the tablecloth.

"Sorry Jane, he didn't mean to hit you!" I yell back over the chaos.

Then I notice the puzzle they chose for this year and I sink in my seat and cover my eyes. "We are screwed," I say, shaking my head. They chose the worst puzzle out of the bunch. The front of the box is a picture of the finished puzzle. Cats. Covered in a bunch of the same colored cats, black and white ones to be exact. They are in all different kinds of poses. Sitting, laying, jumping, and with big, pleading eyes. And of course, because of my week spent sulking, we didn't even practice this one. Even though it was one of the ones I purchased.

"Calm down and concentrate," Dustin says while grouping the pieces in sections.

"How can you be so focused? We didn't even practice this one."

"There is no *we*. *I* practiced it." He starts moving the corners into place and the edges in a section together. I grab a few to help sort, following his method.

I can't believe he practiced. This shocks me. I realize now I may have judged a book by its cover. There's more to the man sitting in front of me. I don't truly know who he is. I thought I did, but I do know he is dedicated to helping me. Whether it's to benefit the farm, or to help my shop. Maybe both.

"We have a first place winner! Congrats to Laura and Chelsea! Everyone else needs to keep solving, don't be discouraged. Try to place within the top five so that you can stay on the leaderboard." Constance is now walking around the tables with a headset and a mini microphone. I don't know where all the upgrades came from, but this year she means business.

Our puzzle only has ten or so pieces left, thanks to Dustin. I have not contributed to even half of the progress that was made.

"Second place goes to Annie and Olive!"

"Third place goes to Mason and Chloe!"

My hands are starting to sweat from the pressure. We need to get at least fifth to keep a spot at a chance to win.

"Fourth place goes to Bobbie and Paula!"

Dustin is laser focused, placing the final piece and we shoot our arms in the air. Constance rushes to our table and shouts "We have a fifth-place winner, Violet and Dustin!"

She taps me on the shoulder. "Good work you two. Just enough to stay on the leaderboard." She's gone in a flash to announce the sixth-place winners and so on. Once everyone is announced she updates us with what the first-place winners receive for finishing the puzzle first. I guess they get to choose two free puzzles from Cat's & Novels. Not that I'm complaining. I don't think I want to look at another puzzle after today. I have every puzzle anyway, but I left them at Dustin's place. Hopefully he keeps them.

"Thank you," I say, looking at Dustin while picking the corners of my fingernail.

"For what?" His eyebrows scrunch.

"For carrying us through this puzzle solving challenge, and for practicing."

He shrugs. "Don't worry about it. I'm doing this for my grandpa. I'm trying to rebuild our strained relationship."

"Oh, okay."

"You didn't have to blow me off this week." His gaze penetrates me to my core. He looks agitated.

"I know. I was busy."

"You keep saying that. But, I'm not buying it. I had to carry this whole competition. We're supposed to be a team, remember?"

"Look—" I start but don't continue.

"It's fine. Call me so we can prepare for next week's competition. If you are going to show up this time."

"I will, but how am I supposed to call you? I don't even have your number."

"Can I have your phone?"

"Sure." I hand him my phone. He swipes across the screen and puts his number in then hands it back to me. On the screen right above his number it says "GRUMPY" in all caps with a chicken emoji. I grin.

"Text me something so I can save your number." I text him some random numbers and hit send. He stares at his phone with a look of concentration, and his fingers fly across the screen. "Here's what I put you in my phone as." I look down and the screen says "fuddy-duddy" with a flower emoji.

"The one and only."

Chapter 15

VIOLET

I feel so bad for blowing Dustin off during the puzzle challenge. So much so I decided to get in my car and drive to his farm. I need to apologize. I didn't want to jeopardize the competition for him. It wasn't his fault at all.

I shut my car off and close the door. It's late in the evening and chilly outside. Good thing I'm still wearing my overalls over my sweatshirt. I knock a few times and wait patiently. I can hear the soft hum of cows mooing in the distance.

"Hey," he says as he notices me standing awkwardly on his doorstep.

I fidget with the sleeves of my sweatshirt. "Can I come in?"

"Yeah. Sure." He opens the door wider for me to enter. I slowly follow him to the couch, grateful to be inside and warm. I sit next to him, crossing one leg over the other. I bounce my knee.

How do I go about this?

He folds his arms over his chest. I can almost feel the tension, it's thick in the air. He's frustrated with me. I can't blame him. I bailed on him. "I'm sorry." I blurt in confession.

"For what?"

"Well. For abandoning you this week. For making you carry the challenge. It was a crappy thing to do."

"It's okay. It's over with." His expression says otherwise.

"No, it's not. There are things I've left unsaid. Things I don't tell anyone. But if you knew. I think you'd understand the reasoning behind why I left."

"Okay, tell me. I'm all ears."

"...Okay, I...there was something you said when I came over. Something that hit me hard. I don't normally think about the past. I try not to." I pause, trying to think about the best way to tell him, without divulging everything. I'm not ready for that. "You said you'd never felt more alone. I agreed with you because...well." I pick at the edge of my overall seams.

Dustin studies me patiently, waiting for me to continue. He doesn't breathe a word. It's comforting.

"I've experienced a lot of grief in my life. I closed myself off from everyone and everything for the week. It wasn't just you...I'm sorry."

"It's okay, you don't have to say more." He reassures me. His features soften. "If I would've known I'd never made a big deal about it. And acted the way I had."

"Truce?" I ask hesitantly.

"Truce."

There's something relieving about being open. Even if it's only a small amount. I'm making strides. They'll be longer and stretch further over time. I will have to break down my walls eventually, but for now I can revel in the little steps I take.

"Does this mean what I think it does?"

"If you mean that we are upgraded to friendship status, then yes. We can be friends now."

"Do you still despise me?"

"A little."

"Good. It makes things more enjoyable."

He grins. "It really does."

"For clarification purposes, there's no best in there? Just friends?"

"That position is already filled."

Why am I jealous all of the sudden?

I shouldn't be; I never get jealous. It's foreign. I don't like it. *What if he has a girlfriend?* The thought passes as quickly as it runs through my mind. Why should I care? We became friends a second ago. It doesn't matter if he has a girlfriend or not.

"Don't look so disappointed. I'm not dating anyone. Nolan and I shared a dorm room in college together and became best friends."

"Oh. I wasn't disappointed." My face suddenly feels warm. I'm sure my cheeks are a rosy hue.

I was never any good at lying. And I'm not any better now.

"Okay. I believe you." *No you don't.* "Ready for next week?"

I sigh. "Yes and no. The competitions get harder each time. It's so exhausting."

"That's true, but at least we won't be arguing anymore."

"Are you confident that we won't be?"

"No. Are you?"

"Nope. Not at all."

Chapter 16

Violet

It's been a slow day in the shop. A few customers have come in looking for some plants, but it's been empty otherwise. I've been spending my free time organizing shelves when my laptop dings with a new email.

Time: Monday, March 11th
From: thornwoodvalleyeventscommittee@email.com
To: violethart@email.com
Subject: Important! Change of plans this Saturday

Dear Small Business Owners of Thornwood Valley,

I hope this email finds you well. There has been a change of plans for this Saturday's competition. Instead of the annual week three pie eating competition, we decided to change things up.

There have been complaints from almost every team about an unfair advantage. The folks that have been participating for many years know what to expect at each competition. This is a valid complaint, so we are doing something about it this year. Instead, there will be a treasure hunt. Each team will be given a total of four clues. You will search the town until every group finds the final treasure. Everyone is to meet at the picnic area between Dr. Newman's office and Fix-Its at one p.m. The String Cheese will have a few tables set up with pizza and pepperoni rolls at noon if you'd like to show up early for a bite to eat.

Please email me with any questions or concerns you may have.

See you soon,
Constance

This is an interesting change of events. I sit back on the stool behind the cash register. I better let Dustin know. I'm sure he hasn't checked his email, since he didn't even know she was sending them in the first place.

> **VIOLET**
>
> Can you believe that email?

To my surprise, he answers almost immediately.

> **DUSTIN**
>
> What email?

> **VIOLET**
>
> Have you been getting any of the emails from Constance?

> **DUSTIN**
>
> No? We've been over this. How would she even get my email anyway?

> **VIOLET**
>
> We're talking about Constance, of course she found your email.

I pocket my phone when Mr. Rhett, Dustin's Grandfather, walks in and to the counter.

"Hi Violet. It's nice to see you." His warm smile lights up the room. He's wearing a pair of jean overalls and work boots.

"Hi Mr. Rhett, what can I help you with?"

"Please call me George. I'd love to get a flower arrangement. I want to surprise Abigail with some for our anniversary tonight."

"Of course. I'm sure she will be so glad to receive them. Do you have anything specific in mind?"

"She always loved roses. Especially white ones."

"Perfect! I have some, I'll grab them for you." My phone buzzes in my pocket while I walk to the flowers stored in the center rack. I walk across them all looking for the rose section.

"How's Dustin treating you?"

I stop and look up at him. I was definitely not expecting that.

"He's been treating me well. We've been making a pretty great team."

"He won't stop talking about you. All I hear while I show him the ropes during the day is about you."

"Really?" I blush, my cheeks turning bright red.

"I only ever tell the truth. I wouldn't make that up. He told me all about the chicken and how it laid an egg on his foot. And how you laughed so hard."

I chuckle. It sure does sound like he knows a lot. "That was the best day ever." My phone buzzes in my pocket again.

"On a more serious note, I've never heard him talk about a love interest ever. Take that how you want."

Love interest? Am I a love interest to Dustin? I thought we were just friends. Anyways, we recently became friends, so there's no way. I find the bouquet of roses and hand them over to George.

"Here you go. I hope Abigail loves them. And happy anniversary," I say with a smile. My phone buzzes in my pocket another time. Who could be texting me so much?

"How much do I owe you?"

"Nothing, this one is on me."

"No dear, you work hard to run this business. Take this." He shoves a bill in my hand, and I know I can't refuse. It won't get me anywhere. "And Violet?"

"Yes?"

"Think about what I said." Before I can ask what he means, he's gone. The shop door swings shut. My phone buzzes again and I'm one centimeter away from throwing the thing out of the window.

DUSTIN

> Oh, there's many emails from her.

> Wait! Change of plans. Is that it?

> Well, I never even knew what the plans were in the first place so I guess this doesn't shock me in the least.

> Are you alive?Was the email too big of a shock? Or are you ignoring me?

VIOLET

> I'm fine. Your grandpa was in the shop. BTW, can you stop blowing up my phone?

DUSTIN

> Self destructing in 3 ... 2 ... 1

VIOLET

> Very funny.

DUSTIN

Meet me tomorrow to come up with a plan of attack for the treasure hunt.

VIOLET

My place at 6. I'll provide dinner.

DUSTIN

It's a date?

VIOLET

It's whatever you want to think it is.

Chapter 17

Violet

Flour covers my clothes. My fingers sting from where I burnt them against the side of the pan. I set the lasagna to cool on the counter and started to make dough for breadsticks and needed some more counter space. Of course, I forgot it was hot and tried to push it over. My burned pointer finger and thumb have my brain to thank for that one. I mumbled profanities under my breath and ran my hand under some cold water which temporarily eased the pain, but now it tingles.

I could have made this whole little "I'll provide dinner text" a lot easier on myself and ordered something from the diner. But I've been in the mood for Italian for weeks, so it was a no-brainer to make something myself. I thought it would be a walk in the park. I always make homemade bread, pasta dishes, and desserts. Olive taught me a lot of her recipes. But the fact that he said lasagna is his favorite food makes me so nervous for his reaction.

I've been a ball of nerves ever since he said, *It's a date?* I know he didn't mean it that way, but I'm getting used to being friends. I wouldn't know how to juggle more.

The timer for the breadsticks goes off and I pull them out of the oven, taking extra care with the oven mitts so that I don't slip up again. The entire spread is finished. Lasagna, breadsticks, a side salad, and my award-winning turtle brownie cheesecake. Okay maybe I'm stretching the truth a little, but Olive thinks that, so it must be, she's an amazing baker.

The clock reads five after six. I plop on the couch to wait. If this were a date, I might have checked in the mirror to fix my crazy hair or changed my clothes to some that aren't covered in flour, maybe even put on my nice jeans. Instead, I am in an oversized purple T-shirt that has an image of a chicken that says, "I may look calm, but in my mind I've pecked you three times." My black leggings are covered in flour dust; I have one sock that is red with chickens on it and another that is yellow with cats on my feet. My apartment is small but efficient. The place is mostly an open concept, the decorating style I was going for was biophilic. The living room and kitchen are connected as soon as you open the door. The island in the kitchen serves as the table, with three bar stools for seating. The couch faces a television in the corner of the room. A bookshelf next to the couch houses hundreds of novels from Cat's & Novel's.

My bedroom is to the back with an ensuite bathroom. The walls all match the fern green downstairs. There are macrame covered hanging baskets everywhere filled with ferns, spider plants, snake grass, and succulents. Plant stands sit in every open corner housing clay pots filled with anthurium, peace lilies, and aloe vera. In the daylight the natural lighting brightens up the space, making it look much larger than it truly is.

A knock sounds on my door. "Come in!" I yell over the song, "Girls Just Want to Have Fun" by Cyndi Lauper in the background. Dustin enters my apartment carrying a cheese tray in his arms. His presence makes me feel at ease. He's dressed in a pair of dark jeans, black tennis shoes, and a corduroy forest green button down. The intro to the song "Careless Whisper" plays in my mind. His face is now covered in scruff that has grown in over the few weeks since I met him. He cleans up nicely, meanwhile I look like I crawled out of a dumpster after deciding to go for a swim in it. Or I could compare my hairstyle to someone who sat in the back of a convertible with their hair down and the wind blew it in every direction for an hour. Then they tried to fix it by putting it in a bun. But it does nothing to make the situation any better. It looks like one big messy clump of hair. "Stupid," I whisper under my breath, praying the ground will swallow me whole.

"What's that?" Dustin says when he makes his way to the love seat across from the couch after setting the tray on my island.

"Oh nothing, just talking to my cat. Fiona, come meet Grumpy," I call out to her. She comes trudging out from the bedroom looking excited.

"I didn't know you had a cat?" he says, bewildered. Like the thought of me taking care of something other than a plant is a shock.

"Yep." My eyes widen when she jumps directly on his lap, purring and nudging her head against his hand. Then she has the audacity to roll onto her back with her belly up. "Traitor." I roll my eyes at the sight. My own cat is crossing to the dark side, and there is nothing I can do about it.

"I can't help it, I'm lovable," he jokes.

"Keep telling yourself that." I roll my eyes.

"So, you want to peck me three times?"

"What?"

"Your shirt. Unless you thought I meant something different, you could do that too." He chuckles and winks.

"Oh, I forgot about the shirt. Absolutely not." My face is completely red from embarrassment.

"Your face tells a different story," he points out.

"Let's eat and discuss a plan of action for the treasure hunt on Saturday." I hop up and slide on my fuzzy camo crocs. Because why not make this look worse while I'm at it?

"I love your outfit. Where did you get the shirt? I want to get one so we can match on our treasure hunt."

"I can't tell if you're being serious or not, but I got everything at Chloe's Closet right next to Rooster's. You know just in case you want the socks, furry crocs, and leggings."

"I'll have to get the leggings when I grab a shirt."

"You know we can't wear just any shirt; it has to at least have our names on the back."

"I'll see what I can do." He grins devilishly. I wonder what he's conspiring.

We make our plates and they are both filled to the brim with steaming food. My mouth waters at the sight.

"Wow. This is delicious. And you remembered this was my favorite," he says while chewing.

"Thanks, I think that was the first compliment you ever gave me. And yes, how could I forget, it was one of the first random facts I learned about you," I say, taking a big bite of a breadstick.

"Don't get used to it. That was a slip up." He chuckles while chewing on more lasagna. "What other random facts did you pick up on?"

"One, you love to solve a puzzle even though you deny it. Two, you have an annoying streak with texting. Three, you're a foodie just like me. Admit it. And four, I think you secretly love it here and don't want to leave."

"Spot on. And of course I am a foodie." He takes a huge bite of lasagna to prove his point. "I figured some things out about you too."

"What's that?"

"You habitually wear messy buns when you're comfortable. Your hair is always falling into your eyes, which aids your proclivity to be clumsy. And you don't let people pass your barriers. Some may try to get close to you, but they don't know what's going on underneath it all. I still don't."

He is spot on. It's all true. A little too true. I do put up my walls with people. I don't like to share everything I'm struggling with. I'd rather put on a smile and keep going.

"You're right." I shrug, twirling my fork between my fingers. "So, about this treasure hunt. What's your plan of attack?" I say between mouthfuls of salad. "I don't think there is a way to plan for something like this."

"Well," he pauses to finish chewing a breadstick. "I think we need to come up with a list of potential clue ideas. Do some research. We can think about how to solve riddles on the spot. So at least we're a little prepared for what is to come."

"I didn't realize you were so good at planning things out," I say while taking a sip of ice water.

"I was an accountant for eight years. So some could say I'm good with numbers, budgeting, and planning. It all sort of compiled together with my experience."

"Oh, I had no clue that's what you did. So, If I ever need small business advice I can come to you?"

"Yeah, I could help. Only because we're friends now. If you asked me a few days ago I would have said no." I chuckle and shove his arm.

We both grab seconds as we continue to chat. And I grab a pen and notebook to jot down ideas as we strategize. This is going to be a long night, but I don't mind it.

"Let's start brainstorming. If you were Constance, what kind of places would you hide things?" I say.

"I don't know why I have this feeling they're going to hide the last clue in the chicken coop."

"Oh! Good point! They always seem to incorporate some type of animal into the mix." I scribble down that idea. "I also have a feeling they might put a clue in my shop, in a flowerpot or something, since all the stores are free range."

"That sounds like something they would do. Especially since there are so many plants. It would take forever to find which one had the clue. It would be almost impossible." He takes a bite of salad as I scribble this idea under another bullet.

"Hey! I don't have that many pots." Dustin gives me a knowing stare. "Okay, I do have a lot of pots and plants."

"Oh. My. God. If I died right now. I would die a happy man. This could be my last meal."

"Dramatic much."

"This is the best cheesecake I have ever put in my mouth," his eyes widen, "but don't tell my grandmother I said that."

"I'll take that as a compliment." I put my fork down on the empty plate. "How old are you? Thirty? I think she can handle it."

"Excuse me, you can't disrespect her cooking like that, not unless you never want to eat it again. She will not take kindly to insults."

I chuckle. "Well then my lips are sealed." I motion to my mouth, zipping it shut.

"Can I have the recipe?"

"Absolutely!"

After a few moments of comfortable silence he asks, "I have a random question, who calls you Vivi? I always hear Olive call you by the nickname. Where did it start from?"

"It's actually not that interesting." I smile, "I guess it had a funny start. Owen (Olive's brother) has a daughter, her name's Octavia. She's two. She couldn't pronounce my name when they brought her into my flower shop. She would call me Vi. And it turned into Vivi. Olive started using the nickname. Everyone picked it up within a few days. They've called me that ever since."

"I like it. Short and sweet. Just like you."

"Aw...shucks. You're making me blush."

His phone starts ringing. The sound breaks through the silence. "I gotta take this, it's my grandpa," he says and I nod. "Hello?—Hello?—Hello?—Hello?" he says into the phone over and over again. "Yes. I'll be home soon. Okay. Bye."

"Is everything okay?"

"Everything is great. He just wanted to make sure I did everything on the list he left me today. He doesn't trust that I can handle it all yet. And I had to wait a few minutes for his phone to connect and it kept going in and out."

"Does his phone not work?"

"It never works. He won't let me set up anything to make the connection better." Dustin taps his chin in deep concentration. "Which gives me an idea. Could you do me a huge favor? If you do this for me, I will owe you big time."

"Depends on the favor. Go ahead."

I think I would do anything he asked at this point. The way he's looking at me could have me melting into a puddle.

"Could you charm my grandparents and keep them distracted for an hour while I set up an antenna on their roof without them finding out?"

"No way, are you kidding? I don't want to be an accomplice to your failed plan and give them a reason to hate me!"

"I promise they won't hate you; if anything, they'll just be mad at me. To be honest I'm just worried that if something happens, they will have no way to call for help if the service doesn't work."

How am I supposed to refuse that? He just wants to keep them safe. "Okay, I'll do it. When?"

"That was easier than I thought. I have to order everything, but as soon as it comes, I'll let you know."

"Okay, I guess I'll be your accomplice."

Dustin and I finish planning and devouring dessert. We chat some more about random things. Mostly about our crazy town and all of the shenanigans the gossip mill pulls. I had a great night hanging out with him. It was rare to relax for an evening and let some of my guards down for the night.

We make our way down to the shop doors in front of the street. The stars contrast against the fading dark sky. Beams of light above each storefront flicker with the change of day to night. Dustin and I stand in front of my shop.

"Bye Vivi." Dustin smirks.

"Bye Dustin."

Chapter 18

VIOLET

I've never noticed how goofy my small town is. While I lounge here, my right leg draped over the left, leaning back on a bench in front of Cat's & Novels, I'm starting to see why the tourist appeal has been increasing.

To my right there's a Rhode Island Red chicken strutting along the sidewalk, pecking in between the cracks. The door to the Hoarder Emporium is wide open, but when I look in, I see floor to ceiling nicknacks and antiques. It's like traveling through time. Hoarder is pretty close to an accurate description, because the place is filled to the brim. I'm waiting for the day Mike and Frank show up from American Pickers. They would be in awe of all of the collectables she has acquired. Then in front of the Chop Shop, Chelsea opens the door waving at me. And starts to walk in my direction. To my horror, Chad follows on her heels.

It was bad enough Jackson cheated with Chelsea; now that Chad is with her too, it's an extra stab in the back.

After a long, busy day filled with customers buying plants to start in their gardens, I am exhausted. And all I want to do is enjoy some fresh air and find a new book to read. I am not ready for whatever these two have planned for me.

"Hey Vivi, it's nice to see you!" She gushes while flipping her long blond hair over her shoulders.

"Hey, it's great to see you too." *No, it's really not.* Not after what she did to my best friend and me in the past. Where's Olive when I need her. Chelsea sits down on the bench next to me. Then Chad follows suit and sits down next to her. He seems to be following her like a lost puppy.

"I hope you're ready to lose this next competition."

Here we go. Be nice Violet. *Be nice.* Don't let the intrusive thoughts in. "On the contrary, I plan to win."

What was that! You were supposed to play it off and not start an argument! I am mentally slapping my face.

"That's rich. You know I've won the past two years. I will be winning again. So just kiss that plaque goodbye," Chelsea says with a snark.

She was and still is a mean girl. In high school, she would always pick on me and Olive. For a while I felt sympathy towards her. I think it comes from her mother. Constance has always been worried about the gossip between everyone else but never gave

Chelsea the light of day. But Chelsea has never shown me a crumb of kindness. I try my best to hold it together, but I'm at my boiling point.

"Hey Violet, are these two bothering you?" Dustin's voice booms from my left. I look up and see him towering over us, looking like a perfect escape plan.

"Not at all. I was just about to tell them I have to go now that you're here. We're going to pick out some books together." I plaster a fake smile on my face, showing my teeth.

"Oh—yeah. That's the plan! Let's go, Vivi. I can't wait to get my hands on those books!" he says, pretending that we were planning to go into the book store together all along.

"Nice chatting with you, Vivi!" I can practically feel the anger emanating from Chelsea's tongue. Chad just sits there silently twiddling his thumbs. And I am so glad Olive and him are over.

I grab Dustin's hand and drag him with me into the store. He stops dead in his tracks when we're inside. He looks bewildered.

"What's wrong?" I question him as he puts a hand up to his mouth.

"I've never been here. I was not expecting this at all." His eyes scan the space up and down.

"And what were you expecting from a store that has 'Cat' in the name?"

"Cat pictures hanging on the walls, cat figurines, a shrine to cats, cat plushies, cat puzzles, but not this—"

His reaction isn't an understatement. Wooden mounted cat trees and shelves span along every open wall. Cat scratching posts, toys, and fake mice are sporadically scattered around the carpet. Then there are so many cats. I think about fifteen strays live here at the moment. The perfume scented cat litter is hard to miss. Ada keeps their litter boxes in the back room and cleans them constantly, but it still wafts out. So, when I buy books I have to air them outside for a few days to get rid of the lingering fragrance, but her prices are hard to beat. Plus, it's the only bookstore for miles. She takes in as many cats as she can until they're adopted. Our rural town has a huge cat breeding problem. That's the great thing about the concept—you can browse a book and take a seat on the chairs behind each aisle, hanging out with the cats. People will adopt them the same day so that they can have a home.

I chuckle and pull him along to the far end of the shelves. A sign points to romance. I scan them all looking for something that intrigues me.

"You don't even seem like this fazes you."

"Not anymore, I'm used to it. Even though it's a touch unconventional. It turned out to be a great idea. Finding a home for many cats. I adopted Fiona here." I pull out a book that looks interesting. "We can find you one if you want."

"I'm good. I don't need any cats. We already have a litter that's living in the barn."

"Suit yourself," I say while choosing a few more books, stacking them on my arm. "I thought you couldn't wait to get your hands on some books?" I ask, repeating what he said earlier.

"Ha! No, I don't have much time for reading, but it seemed like you needed to be saved from that conversation. Especially after what you told me the other day. The look in your eyes was pure rage. I had to do something before you did something you might regret."

"I wasn't that angry." My eyes meet his and then dart away quickly.

"Keep telling yourself that and maybe you'll believe it." A white and gray kitten brushes up against his leg. He bends down to pick it up and starts to pet it. The kitten starts purring immediately, snuggling against his arms. My heart melts.

"My name is Sardine, please take me home." He reads the kitten's collar out loud.

"You should get him! His name is so cute! Look, he already loves you."

After arguing for five minutes on whether he needs a cat or not, I end up purchasing three books when only coming in for one. Sardine follows Dustin to the register and tries to follow him out the door. To my dismay, he leaves empty handed.

"I'm going to head back to the farm before it's dark. I have some more work to finish for the day."

"I might as well get going too." I open the door and swing my shopping bag back and forth.

"I'll meet you at your place tomorrow before we make it to the picnic area, around noon." He winks then walks to the parking lot and hops in his grandpa's truck.

I wonder what that was all about.

Chapter 19

DUSTIN

The weather in Pennsylvania is bipolar. Yesterday was sunny and sixty-five degrees. The perfect weather for being outside. Today is a crisp forty-five degrees with rain. The worst possible weather for doing anything outside. I hope it clears up by tomorrow for the scavenger hunt. I doubt it will.

I shut the SUV ignition off. Water droplets streak down my windshield one after another, a race to make it to the hood first.

Don't ask me why I drove into town to walk over to Cat's & Novel's. I was *never* a cat person. If I were to get any type of pet, I would have gotten a dog—likely a lab, golden retriever, or some other type of large dog breed. But I still can't get over the defeated look in Violet's eyes when I said no to the kitten. I don't need a cat. I don't have time for a cat. Okay, I'm lying, cats aren't really that time consuming. Also, that kitten gave me the most disappointing look yesterday. His eyes got all big and sappy and it ripped my heart out to leave him there. Damn, the sad looks from both Violet and Sardine were enough to kill a man. And that's why I'm going back in.

What kind of name is Sardine anyway?

After spending the hour filling out papers, I walk out of the shop holding my new litter box, food, toys, cat scratching stand, and a bunch of other random item's the shop owner piled on my arms. I barely paid anything, they just kept adding on more and more for free. I shove everything into the back of my car. I walk back into the store and pick up Sardine. He starts meowing the instant I walk in the door. I pick him up and carry him down the street. Doing my best to shield him from the rain. I am in over my head with this decision. I don't know what's gotten into me.

I walk across the street to the NSSG to find Violet behind the counter helping a customer. She's so engrossed in their conversation that she doesn't even notice me walk in. I sit on the green couch not far from the counter. Sardine lays across my lap, purring incessantly. I guess somebody is glad about my decision, but he sure seems to be happy to be here. My phone buzzes from my pocket with a text. I pet Sardine while I read the message.

NOLAN

How's farm life coming along?

Still the same as when we talked last. Great. How's NYC treating you?

I'm living large in your old apartment. Oh, btw I'm coming to visit next weekend for your final competition. Send me the details, I'll see you then, Farmer.

"You got Sardine!" Violet shrieks and runs to greet him.

"I guess I did." I still can't believe it.

I slide my phone into my jeans' pocket and lean against the back of the couch with a smug grin.

"Three questions. One, did you really get him? Two, what made you change your mind? Three, oh my god, you got him!"

"Yes. I felt bad for the kitten, so I went back to get him—I'm not heartless. Your third one wasn't a question." I hand Sardine over.

"You know what I mean." She sighs at me, then proceeds to whisper loving words to the kitten like he's the best thing in the world. I never thought I'd be so jealous of a cat.

"Do you want to go to my place and help me set up his new home?"

"Yes! Absolutely! I'm so excited. This is the best day ever. I'm closing the shop, that customer just left. I don't care."

"Calm down." I chuckle.

"I can't! Look at him. He's the cutest little guy I've ever seen. Aren't you, Sardine?" Her voice goes up an octave. She scratches behind his ears and he continues purring.

After turning off the lights and locking up she gets in the car with me. Her leg bounces with anticipation. Sardine sits on her lap sleeping.

I can't believe I almost never adopted him.

Her hair is damp with beads of rain. She's wearing her signature overalls over a sweatshirt. She shivers.

"Are you cold?"

"A little."

"I can see your teeth chattering." I say as I turn up the heated seats. I angle the vents towards her and crank them up too.

"That's much better." She sighs. Her eyes close.

By the time I pull in the driveway. They're both sleeping. I want to take a picture of this moment. They look so peaceful. I wouldn't dare wake either of them.

I shut off the engine and she stirs. Stretching her arms. Sardine copies her and stretches his paws out on her lap.

Violet smiles, "He's adorable."

"I know." *You are too.* I want to say, but don't.

"The front doors unlocked. I'll bring everything in. Make yourself at home."

"Thanks," she exits my car and scurries inside with Sardine.

I carry the mounds of cat related items into the dining room and set it all on the table. I save the cat scratch post for last. I put it in the corner of the room. "Is this good here?"

"Yes. Perfect. You should put the litter box in your basement if you have one."

"I do. That's a good idea." After setting up everything. Sardine runs around my house. It didn't take long for him to feel right at home. He jumps through the air chasing the fake mice attached to a wand. He looks like he's doing acrobats in my living room. Violet lights up every time he grabs a new toy. Soon the floor is covered in feathers, mice, yarn, and tiny little balls.

Those are going to hurt like hell when I step on one in the middle of the night.

In no time we're all leaning back on the couch. Sardine lays between us. Eyes closed, belly up. Soft snores escape his little body.

"That was really sweet of you." Violet says quietly.

"What was?" I ask.

"Going back there and getting him. I'm so glad you did."

"Me too." I meant it wholeheartedly.

Chapter 20

VIOLET

It's dreary today. Normally I wouldn't mind a good rain storm. The noise it makes while hitting a metal roof is like music to my ears. And how it waters grass and plants. Everything grows so beautifully after a storm.

Normally I wouldn't be running around town like a chicken with its head cut off.

I cover my face with my palm. My thoughts are *dark* today. That wasn't funny. *Sorry Helga.* I whisper, as if she could hear me through my shop. I swivel on the barstool staring at my plants. Nobody's in here today. I had a measly four customers come in. I don't know why I bothered opening. I guess to keep myself busy.

The bell chimes and Dustin comes in. He shrugs his rain coat on the rack and turns to face me.

"Oh my God, your sweatshirt!" I shriek.

"Do you like it?" He grins.

"Do I like it? I love it! How did you get it so last minute?"

"I pulled some strings with Chloe. She expedited this one for me. But don't worry, I had one made for you too. Here." He hands me a bag that says "Chloe's Closet" on the front. I pull out the dark purple sweatshirt with the saying, "I may look calm, but in my mind I've pecked you three times."

This is the best thing anyone's ever gotten me.

My eyebrows shoot up as I examine the sweatshirt. I flip it over to see my name printed on the back. I throw it over my t-shirt and spin. "How do I look?" I giggle.

He pauses, voice cracking when he says, "ready for battle."

Sometimes things are unexpected in life. Nothing ever really goes to plan. Dustin showing up with the sweatshirt was a happy unexpected thing. The sky dropping down with rain was *not* a happy unexpected thing. And when I say dropping, I'm not kidding. Pelting rain drops pour over us, pounding across the ground in splashes. We are soaked. All itching for this competition to start so that we can get inside to feel warmth. I'm ready for this day to be over.

All of the groups are huddled under the only pavilion in town. Everyone sits in the center of picnic tables munching on pizza, breadsticks and pepperoni rolls, courtesy of The String Cheese. At least something good came out of participating today. Poor Daisy is stuck out here in the rain with us. She keeps the tables stocked with food and changes out empty boxes. She doesn't seem to mind though. I think she's just excited to get out of the shop for a day, and she loves to watch the competitions.

I take a bite of a bread stick as I look around at the teams all congregating. Olive and Annie are chatting, looking focused, probably planning strategy. They've been making a comeback from last year. And have a shot at winning this year.

Constance is chatting with her husband, Chuck, sitting in the far corner. Megaphone in hand. She looks as if she's getting ready to make an announcement. The rain pours around us, not letting up in the slightest. I toss my plate in a trash can next to our table when I hear the static. "Everyone, five minutes until we start. A little rain won't stop us from continuing. Just be careful; the sidewalks are slick." Her voice booms across the crowd.

"Your first clue is lined up on the long table on my right. Each color envelope correlates to your team colors. One member should grab it within the next few minutes. You know the drill, here are the rules. Rule number one, don't open the envelope until I say go. Rule number two, no sabotaging other teams by hiding their clues. At one o'clock the teams should all line up along the front of the pavilion so that no one has an unfair advantage. Don't forget every team has a different set of clues and trophy to find. Your trophy has your team name on it, so you can't steal someone else's and claim it as your own." Her voice dies down and the static shuts off.

"I'll grab our envelope," Dustin says and walks off.

I'm so nervous. I don't know if it's the fact that I realize I'm super clumsy and I'm most definitely going to wipe out at some point today. Or the fact that the man sitting next to me is starting to make me feel like I have butterflies in my stomach when I'm around him. It's becoming harder to fight the attraction. I hope it's not one sided.

A few minutes later, Dustin sits next to me, armed with the purple envelope. I shiver from the frigid air; I can feel the cold down to my bones. After waiting for what feels like forever, we finally make our way to the front of the pavilion to line up with the other small business owners.

Constance counts down the seconds, "Three, two, one, go!"

Everything is a chaotic blur. Teams are running past us out of the pavilion. Others stand in place, ripping open their envelopes. Dustin and I planned to stay put and read the first clue, so that we could figure out where to look first. Running blindly wouldn't help us in the least. He tears into the corner and unfolds a white piece of paper.

"You can find me where the mini trees are," Dustin reads the clue out loud. "I have no clue what that means—mini trees? Does The Hoarder Emporium or Cat's & Novel's sell mini tree figurines? Or does our town have a Christmas tree farm I don't know about?"

"We do! Olive's parents have one. But they wouldn't put it that far out of town. It has to be within walking distance." I scratch my head. "Wait, I know!" I grab Dustin's hand and tug him with me. My hand tingles with nervous tension against the touch, but I don't have much time to think about it. We slide along the sidewalk passing a few shops. At this point my hair is drenched so it sticks to my neck. I continue to blow my bangs out of my eyes. When they're wet they become a nuisance. I should have pinned them up before this competition. I've also slipped a few times already, but Dustin caught me every time. I'm just glad I settled on wearing a pair of rain boots with good grips on the bottom.

Suds in the Bucket car wash carries the scented mini trees for cars. Right along the wall they have a dispenser and if I'm guessing correctly, the next clue should be there.

"Why in the world are we at the car wash?" Dustin asks in between huffs of breath.

"You'll see, unless I'm wrong." The car wash is deserted. Most of the townies seem to stay out of town during events, or hang out grabbing food and watching the competitions. But who would be at the car wash right now anyway? It's raining. The building has four open bays, each one equipped with a sprayer nozzle and brush. It's the old-fashioned self-serve system that you put quarters in to add time. Sure enough at the outer building wall there is a tree air freshener dispenser. Another purple envelope is taped to the side.

"You are a genius!" Dustin shouts through the pouring rain. He grabs the next clue and hands it to me to read.

"Why, thank you." I bow, teasing him. I unfold the envelope and start reading, "Congratulations! You found me. But don't get too *cocky*. You might have to *cluck* your way to the next one."

"It's in the chicken coop, isn't it?"

"Unfortunately." I shrug.

Chapter 21

DUSTIN

The next clue was taped to the inside of the chicken coop. All of the chickens are perched inside for the day, ducking in to escape the rain. I can't blame them. Thankfully, Mason keeps the inside clean, fresh hay lines the floors, so it isn't as bad as I was expecting. It's actually nice to be out of the rain, even if it's for only a few minutes. Violet is crouching down petting Miss. Helga, our good luck charm. Let's hope she can spread some of that luck for us today, because we need it to make it through this scavenger hunt.

"Good job, you found the second clue. To find the next one follow the stone path to a pool of blue. I'm on the side of something standing, feet grounded."

"The pond—it has to be. But what's the thing standing?" Violet scratches her head in thought while looking at the chickens.

What could it be?

I've gone for a few runs on the path that leads to the pond and one thing sticks out to me the most. "The bulletin board with the news and town map. Its posts are anchored in concrete."

"Yes! It has to be!" Violet hops up and pulls me into a squeezing hug. Her arms envelope me in her grip. I hug her back; the electricity of our connection doesn't go unnoticed. But before I can comment on it, she's running from the coop behind the shops, bee-lining it to a path hidden between trees. Instead of backtracking to the town sidewalk we run through the woods behind the shops. It's a muddy mess. I follow her, weaving in and out of trees. I would lead her so that I can be the one to fall first if something's in the way, but I haven't been through this part of the town before. So, I would just hold her back.

Soon enough the woods part to a clearing with the pond in the center. Like a beacon of blue, the trees reflect on the water's surface. The sign is not too far from where the woods meet the opening. Before I have a chance to keep running, Violet starts to tumble to the ground, falling headfirst into a thick patch of mud. It happens in a blur. Her arms flail out in front of her on instinct to catch the fall. But she's too slow and ends up fully covered. She lays there for what feels like hours. I run to her side, hoping that she's okay. Fear shoots through me.

Screw the challenge. The thought crosses my mind. All I care about is her. I couldn't care less about winning, or anything else. I just need her to be okay.

She rolls onto her back. Her face is covered in mud, her sweatshirt and jeans caked in brown.

"Vivi. Are you okay?" I ask, my voice filled with concern. I kneel down to make sure she's alright. Feeling déjà vu all over again. She is a glutton for falling.

"Can—you help me up?" she mumbles, stretching out her right hand up to me. I grab it and start to pull her up. She tugs on me so hard that the shock makes me lose my balance. My feet give out and I tumble into the mud beside her. She explodes into a fit of giggles, turning to look at me while we both laugh. Lying in a heap of mud, all of the worries I've been letting sit in the back of my mind fade away. Being laid off a few weeks ago. Also throwing in the fact that I am now running a farm, not knowing if it's what I want to do for the rest of my life. If someone told me a few weeks ago that I'd be happier than I've been in years living here in Thornwood Valley, laying in a patch of mud, weeks spent entertaining the town's competitive small business games and now a proud owner of a cat named Sardine, with Violet by my side, I would have laughed in their face and called them a liar. But now that I'm here looking into Violet's warm eyes that sparkle against the pouring rain, I can't help but feel like I'm finding myself for the first time.

I don't know how long we've been lying here, listening to the tree branches sway. Or how long I've been scanning her face. The crimson flush of cheeks against pale, mud painted skin.

The magnetic pull draws me in, a force stronger than I can control. We are merely inches away from each other. The heat radiates from our close proximity against the chill outside. We're so close that her shampoo fills my senses with hints of chamomile and bergamot. The sweet scent permeates me, I don't ever want to forget it. Lost in the moment a thought crosses my mind. I want to brush my lips against hers so I can find out what they would feel like against mine. Would they be soft and warm? Does she feel the magnetic pull between us as much as I do?

Her eyes flutter closed, a silent invitation.

A loud crash of thunder sounds in the sky.

Dammit.

It makes Violet and I come to our senses.

Chapter 22

VIOLET

I have no words. I'm completely and utterly speechless. I brush my hands against my lips and my cheeks are flushing a bright crimson. I just know it. I can't believe we were so close to kissing. I was not expecting that at all. As the rain drops sizzled against my cheek, like cool drops of water against a hot electric stove, steaming against the surface from the sudden impact, his light blue eyes saw directly into my soul.

"Stay here, I'll grab the clue." Dustin says and I shake the thoughts from my head.

"No, I'm going." I huff in frustration.

"Please? I don't want you to fall."

"Okay, I'll stay." My eyes go to my feet. Even though at this point, there's not much more damage I could do. I am covered in mud head to toe. It's caked in my hair, all over my clothes, and on my face. People pay good money for a mud treatment that I just got for free. I laugh to myself.

"Want to hear the next clue?" Dustin holds the last envelope that leads to the final treasure. Once we find the last one, we have to take it to the pavilion. I nod my head up and down in agreement. "Congratulations, this is your final clue to the treasure. You can find me somewhere where there are tons of things stacked and piled. I am at the top in a box. You'll know what kind of box when you see it. Happy hunting."

"Jane has a serious collecting problem," Dustin grunts while he opens another empty box at the top of the stacks of items in The Hoarders Emporium. "You weren't kidding when you said it's exactly as described. I thought you were exaggerating to make me sweat about finding this box." He balances on a tall, rickety wooden ladder. I'm on the ground trying my best to hold the thing in place. It's swaying back and forth every time he moves.

This isn't going to end well.

"Woah." The ladder sways a little too far and almost tips him off the side.

"Sorry!" I shout, balancing it back flush.

"Be honest, are you trying to kill me? If you hated me, you could just tip the ladder and I'd be a goner."

"I never hated you Grumpy. You won't know when it's coming anyway. Expect the unexpected."

"That's nice to know." He chuckles. He continues to open a few more boxes, but each one comes up empty. Out of the corner of my eye something shines.

"I saw something sparkle up there a few boxes back! Check around there."

"That's it! It's a treasure chest!" Dustin yells, his voice is breathy, and he must be exhausted. The chest is a faded wood with gold trim edges. A lock is on the front and I'm praying it isn't latched. He steps down the ladder and hands me it. "You do the honors; I'm ready for a nap."

Thankfully the lock wasn't closed. As I open it up it creaks to reveal a custom trophy shaped like a rooster. In small cursive engraved in the bottom it says, *2024 Thornwood Valley Small Business Games Participant.* I take a moment to admire how neat it is. "Let's go." I grab his hand, and my fingers intertwine with his. We run as fast as we can through town. The rain has settled down, but at this point I'd be glad if it didn't so that this mud could wash off me. We did our best to try to keep from tracking mud into the antique shop by taking our shoes off at the door, but we still managed to cover the floor. Jane will thank me later. I'm sure I'll be back scrubbing the floors later on today.

As we make it back to the pavilion, my heart drops. It looks like some teams already made it back. Olive, Annie, Chelsea, and Laura are already eating cold pizza. I cost us this one with my fall.

"Congrats you two! You are in third place, so you made it to the next round! First place won ice cream at Bobbie's freeze tonight. I take it you're not too disappointed about missing that. You both look freezing. And why are you covered in mud?" Phew! For a moment there I thought we lost. I'm surprised we made it in time.

"Don't ask." I sigh and grab a piece of cold pizza. I shove as much as I can in my mouth.

Olive smirks looking back and forth from me to Dustin. She averts her gaze at our joined hands that I forgot were intertwined. I release his hand swiftly. That's not what I was going for. I held it when running. So that I didn't fall. I shake my head at her and roll my eyes.

"Did you just have a full-on conversation with Olive without saying anything?" Dustin's voice whispers into my ear.

"Yeah, we did."

"How do girls do that? Do you have telepathy or something?" he asks, looking perplexed. He looks back and forth between us trying to figure out what we just said.

"If I told you all of my secrets it wouldn't be any fun." I shrug.

Maybe I do want to tell him all my secrets. It would be nice to confide in someone. But I'm worried he will run when he finds out the truth.

And that's what scares me more than anything. I don't want to be alone again. Although I have Darcy and Olive, it's nice to have another friend to talk to.

But sharing everything is too risky. So, for now I'm keeping it all to myself.

Chapter 23

VIOLET

"Who are you?" Darcy looks at me with her eyebrows furrowed. She's lying in bed today, watching *The Golden Girls* on the television. I can hear the muttering of Blanche and Rose arguing over something silly. The sight makes me feel a little relieved that she remembers her favorite show. Even if it's only something small.

Today must be a bad day. I was hoping that it would be a good one. I wanted to tell her all about Dustin and me becoming friends. I needed to confide in her. I'm still scared to share my heart with someone after what happened with my last relationship. I thought she would have advice, because she always knows what to say.

"Oh, I know who you are! Lily, it's so good to see you. I missed you dear! How is my sweet Violet?" My stomach drops to my feet. Days like these hurt. She does this every so often where she mistakes me for my mom. It's too hard to correct her though, because it makes her frantic trying to explain that Lily is gone. So I usually just play along, instead of reintroducing myself. It's for the best.

"It's good to see you too Darcy. Violet is doing well."

"Oh, I am so glad to hear it. I love that girl. When are you going to bring John and her to visit?" My heart breaks again at the mention of my dad.

"Sometime soon, I promise." I wish I could bring them in to visit.

"Have a seat, please. Have a seat honey."

"I can't stay long, but I just wanted to make sure you were doing okay. What did you have for dinner today?"

"They gave me meatloaf and green beans. I hate meatloaf, who enjoys that anyway? I'd rather starve."

"I can go get you something from the diner?"

"No, it's no bother. I ate it, I just didn't like it. Sometimes we have to suck it up and hope for something better the next day."

"Fingers crossed you get some type of chicken tomorrow, you always love that."

"Wouldn't that be a dream."

"Okay, well I guess it's time for me to go. I love you, Darcy."

"I love you, Lily. Don't forget to tell Violet and John I love them too."

"I will."

"Promise me you'll bring them in to see me tomorrow. I miss them. *Please* promise," she says with determination.

"I promise." My voice breaks. I don't like to make promises I can't keep, but this promise is one I have to make so that I don't hurt her.

I just end up hurting myself instead.

Chapter 24

VIOLET

*M*y eyes flicker open. The blackness slowly fades, and the bright light burns my eyesight. There is a person standing in front of me, but I can't make out who it is. Everything is a blur of foggy, unrecognizable shapes. I blink a few times to focus on who it is. "Mom?" My voice croaks.

"No, honey—it's Ms. Burton from the flower shop," the woman says in a concerned tone. My eyesight is clearing and sure enough, she's the only one in the room with me. It's a small room with light blue walls. I'm lying down. My arm is hooked to an IV. My body is numb, but I don't feel any pain. Black and blue splotches cover my arms and exposed legs. A bright pink cast covers my left leg. I examine my arm and notice a long white bandage covering it. A few more bandages cover my other leg and arm.

What happened to me?

"Where am I?" I ask Ms. Burton. I'm glad to see her familiar face looking back at me. But her eyes are puffy and unfocused. I can tell she was crying.

"You are in a hospital in Virginia."

"What happened? Why am I here? Where are Mom and Dad?"

"Honey, there's something I have to tell you." Her eyes glisten with fresh tears.

Then it hits me like a bitter revelation. I remember everything before my vision went black.

I wake up with tears in my eyes. It was just a dream. It was just a dream. I repeat the words through a loop in my mind, willing them to be true.

I wish it was just a dream. Today was the day I lost everything, and the painful reminder eats at me every year.

I grab the purple notebook on my nightstand hoping for a semblance of something happy. I open to a random journal entry.

Dear H,

Today was one of the worst days of my life. When I received the call, I was in shock. It was all so much worse than I could have imagined. Lily and John are gone. How can they be gone? They are so much younger than me. I was supposed to go first. Not them. Nothing is right in the world. This can't be true. Sadly, it is. Poor Violet is barely hanging on. I'm with her now in the hospital waiting for her to wake up. What am I going to tell her? How do I make it sound like there is hope? At the moment I don't believe in any hope myself. I have to be strong for her. I am all that she has. I love her and I would do anything for her; she's just like a granddaughter to me. She's only fifteen and her parents are gone. This doesn't feel real. I wish that you could be by my side as more than a friend, but I don't want to ruin our friendship so I can't give you this letter. But I know you will be there for me regardless.

With Love,
Darcy Burton

The letter I chose was not what I was hoping for. How can it be that the next entry is the last one I needed to read at that moment?

I tug my white, flower-covered duvet comforter off me, the decorative tassels swaying as it lands on the end of the bed with a thump. I throw on a pair of leggings, a sports bra, and pull my hair up into a high ponytail. A sweatshirt from the day before calls to me from the floor. That will have to do. I drape it over my body and shove on some running shoes.

I take the stairs two at a time and run into a storage closet in the shop, grabbing my collapsible fishing rod and kit. I shove it into a drawstring bag and throw it over my shoulders, then skid straight out the door.

I run on the sidewalk along the town, heading straight for the pond behind some of the shops. It's still dark and I can barely see in front of me. The soft glow from the streetlights leaves a small path of sight. I'm running as if I'm being chased.

It was all my fault. The thought haunts me. I never knew what I had until it was all gone. In the blink of an eye everything that I had taken for granted disappeared. Leaving me cold and broken. Alone and guilt stricken. I can never forgive myself.

I made it to the opening of the trail in record time. I run with a purpose down the path that leads straight to the pond. It's a straight shot from here on.

The sky is starting to lighten, but there are no streetlights on this stretch of path. So, I'm running blindly. My feet are moving and my eyes are filled with tears. I can barely feel my legs anymore. I see what looks like a dark shadow moving towards me. My eyes must be playing tricks on me because there is no way anyone is out here this early in the morning.

Before I have a chance to move out of the way, I slam straight into what feels like a brick wall. Stars flood my vision as I fall backwards. I'm inches from hitting the stone path when strong arms grab my waist and break my fall.

I either ran straight into a serial killer or I'm imagining things. Probably and *hopefully* the latter.

"Are you okay?" a male voice disrupts my thoughts.

I know that voice. It's a voice I've heard for the past three weeks. One I thought I loathed and now I somehow feel comfortable around. My thoughts are a whirlwind of emotions. He saved me from falling this time? I feel like all I do is make a fool out of myself around him. I'm constantly clumsy in his presence.

"Violet, what happened?" he asks again, concerned.

That does it. Hearing him worried for me opens the floodgates of my emotions. I haven't let anyone in my life for years, other than Olive and Darcy. And I don't share much with them anymore. They've done more than enough for me in the past. These feelings are the ones I've been holding onto for so long. Not once did I allow myself to face anything head on. Not since the day my life stopped. I work constantly to try and keep my mind busy, running the shop, helping other store owners, always busy. I haven't let myself have a break to feel my emotions.

Just say you're fine. "No—I'm not okay." I croak and my body sags into him. He wraps an arm around me, pulling me to a bench along the path.

"Hey, did I hurt you? I'm so sorry if I did." He looks at me, checking for injuries, and brushes tears from my face. "I can call Dr. Newman. I'm sure she'd see you this early." He pulls out his phone to call her.

"No, don't call Paula. You didn't hurt me. I'm physically fine." My voice cracks and comes out scratchy.

Sobs rake my body, and I shake uncontrollably. At some point in my catatonic state Dustin takes off my drawstring bag and pulls me into his arms. They are strong and hold me steady. Like a weighted blanket draping over my body keeping me safe.

We don't talk for what feels like hours. My head is leaning against his chest. His hand brushes soothing strokes up and down my back. My tears have subsided, but the bone deep ache is still there, festering.

He remains quiet, not a single word spoken. Although he didn't ask, I feel as if I owe him some sort of explanation. I owe it to myself. I want to tell him. "Thirteen years ago today my parents and I were on our way to North Carolina to go to Nags Head." My voice is almost a whisper, but Dustin doesn't move, he just continues holding me. "We got into a car accident halfway through our trip. I was the only one who made it. A drunk driver hit our car."

"I'm so sorry Violet. You don't owe me an explanation. If you don't want to tell me anything more, you don't have to," he says, looking down at me. His ocean blue eyes look into mine with a somber expression and I soften. His dirty blonde hair is tousled and his shirt is tear soaked.

"I want to explain." I wipe a stray tear from my left eye. "That's why I won't drink alcohol. I know it had nothing to do with me, but I won't touch it regardless. Someone drinking took away everything I had. I can't bear to touch it."

Dustin shakes his head. "I'm sorry I ever asked. I shouldn't have."

"No. It's okay. You were asking a harmless question. I just wanted to explain."

I will tell him everything eventually, but right now I'm glad to be able to feel comfort. It feels good to get it off my chest. I trust him.

"I'm so sorry about your shirt."

"That is the least of my concerns."

Chapter 25

DUSTIN

Tiny droplets of morning dew glisten against the oncoming sunrise, sparkling rivulets covering the green grass and maple leaves. The chorus of robins chirping fills my ears, with a sense of warmth. Splash! The water ripples across the pond surface as Violet's hook makes contact. I take a sip of coffee from my right hand while balancing a fishing rod in the other. We sit in silence, waiting for the first fish to bite.

An hour ago, we walked back to the NSSG and grabbed some coffee in her apartment. She also grabbed a container of worms out of the mini fridge. Apparently, she keeps them in stock in case anyone wants some to go fishing at the pond. I asked if I could join her fishing and she said, "Of course." It was too early to go to the coffee shop after our four o'clock run in. I didn't think she would want to go there anyway, at least not yet. I know it was hard for her to tell me and I didn't want to leave her alone. I had no clue her parents passed away. Or that she was in the accident that took their lives.

It's tragic. And my heart breaks for her. It's my fault I didn't know any of this about her already; I should have asked more questions. I should have tried to get to know her on a deeper level, but then again it wasn't my place to ask. I always knew there was something bothering her. I wanted to give her time to tell me on her own terms.

I've never experienced loss in my life. Both of my parents still live in Philadelphia. We get along well, but it's a distant relationship. I see them maybe once a year. I'm the closest to my grandparents. Although I haven't seen the farm in years, they visited me in New York once a year. We also talk on the phone regularly. On Christmas we all get together with my parents, my sister and a few cousins who I haven't seen in years.

If I knew the right words to say or understood how she was feeling I'd say more. But there isn't anything I know to comfort her with, and is there really any right thing to say? So, I decided that I'm going to be here for her. At least as long as she needs me today, so she won't be alone in her thoughts.

"Why were you out here so early in the morning? Were you spying on me?" She chuckles.

This woman is so incredibly strong, to still make jokes through all of the pain. I know it's her coping mechanism. A way to cover up the bad with a little bit of laughter. She doesn't need to joke to hide how she truly feels around me. I just want her to feel comfortable enough to be honest with me. Although, I dug my own grave the first day we met. I'm hoping to show her over time that I will be there for her.

I want to be the one there for her.

"Well, I was spying on the other teams so that we'd have a better chance at winning the last competition." I lean back against the wooden bench and set my coffee down in the holder.

"Really?" She looks at me, her hazel eyes opened in shock.

"No! Of course not. Who would be up this early? I was running. Hoping to get some exercise in. Grandpa said this next competition is supposed to be some kind of sport."

"Oh, that makes more sense. If you do need some help spying just give me a call next time and I'll be there."

"I will, don't you worry," I tease.

"Fish on!" she yells when the rod tugs her forward. The top of the rod bends downward; she holds it up while reeling and tugging backward. "It has to be a big one!" I can't help but notice the smile that spreads across her face. She reels the rod in while continuing to fight the fish. I try to help her, but she insists she's good. After what feels like forever, she finally lands the fish. And to her horror it is the smallest bluegill we've both ever seen.

A FOWL MATCH

I hold my hand across my face trying so hard not to break out into laughter. She beats me to it by laughing. Then we're both laughing our asses off.

"I don't think this one's a keeper." She takes it off the hook as she wipes a bead of sweat off her forehead, then leans down to release it back into the water.

"Wait! Let me take a picture." I pull out my phone and she poses with it, wearing a huge smile. Then she releases it back into the water, cupping it to let it swim gently out of her hands.

"My parents both loved to fish," she says all of a sudden, grabbing a worm and putting it on the hook. Then she casts it back into the water. "They would take me almost every weekend right here. It became a tradition. I come here to fish just to remember them. To remember all of the good times." She sits back down, crossing her legs.

"That's really nice that you can come here to remember. I'm glad that you let me be here with you," I say sitting back down too.

"Ms. Burton paid to have this bench put here with a plaque for them when I was younger. We always used to bring folding chairs, but she wanted me to have a special place to visit." She reels in her line a little. "She was really close with my mom. My mom worked at the shop when she was in between jobs. So that's why she was the one who took care of me after they passed. I had no one else. I worked for her at the flower shop before the accident. So afterwards she became everything to me. The NSSG was passed on to me two years ago as a gift from her. Then she moved into the retirement home, though I insisted she live with me. Her dementia was getting worse, so she decided it was time. It's just me now. Even though I visit her weekly it's not the same. I feel alone in the world. Especially on the days her memory is bad, and she doesn't remember me. So you see why I understand what feeling alone is like. I'm sorry I'm rambling. I don't know why I'm telling you all of this." She scratches her head, looking down at her lap.

I tilt her chin and lift her head. "Do not apologize. I don't mind being here or listening. You're not alone anymore—you have me."

Something has shifted between Violet and me. And I can't stop finding excuses to be with her.

Chapter 26

VIOLET

"Baaaaa." My new friend speaks to me as I pet her head. Dustin has been holding out on me this whole time. They have goats on the farm. And they are adorable. They are the perfect distraction. It's exactly what I needed today. I was planning on spending the rest of the day in bed, rather than trying to do anything productive. After we spent the morning fishing he took me to the Rhett Family Farm. We rode around in the side-by-side while he gave me a tour of everything. First, we stopped by the barn to see some calves. They were adorable and he had to practically drag me out of there, promising that I can stop by anytime I want. Then we rode around the fields taking in the beautiful scenery, while checking all of the fences since his grandpa had a list of things for him to do. And now we're at our last stop for the day in the goat barn.

"So, what do you do with the goat's milk?" I ask while petting my favorite one some more. Her name is Little Miss. She is a beautiful black, brown, and white Nigerian Dwarf goat. Her fur is soft and smooth to the touch, she's extremely docile.

"Gram uses the milk to make cheeses, soap, lotions, and even dehydrates some too. She begged my grandpa to get some goats for years and he finally caved. Even though he takes care of them. She uses all of the milk and makes things for us. It's more of a hobby for them at the moment." He scoops some pellets and drops them into a trough. "Little Miss has been producing milk for about half a year after kidding. But we have to make sure that she's milked regularly. So that she keeps producing."

"She doesn't sell anything that she makes?"

"No, she just trades it for eggs and gives it out around town. But I'm thinking about breeding some more goats and producing larger batches of milk so that we can expand the farm's business. Maybe I could start selling it at Valley Harvest. They already offer local honey, milk, and syrup. I think the goat cheeses would do well."

"That's such a good idea! You'd have me as a customer. I love goat cheese. Also, I need some of this soap and lotion as soon as possible."

"I'm sure Gram will send you home with a bag of goodies after dinner tonight."

That's news to me. I didn't know I was joining them for dinner. I was not expecting to stay. I really don't want to step in on their family dinner. But I haven't had a home cooked meal that wasn't of my own making in years so the idea is very tempting. "Are you sure I can join? I don't want to be a bother."

Looking agitated at my indecision he says, "You are not a bother at all, my gram will be giddy at the prospect of a girl at dinner. Believe me, she will be trying to add you to the family by the end of the night. Anyways, she always makes enough food to feed an army. I called her earlier to let her know you'd be joining us. Hoping you would say yes."

I would love that. I've been missing being part of a family for so long.

"You didn't exactly ask me, you just proclaimed I was going." I shrug my arms across my chest. I smirk, knowing I would have gone either way.

"I didn't want to give you the chance to say no—" He shrugs. "You promised me that favor and I'm cashing in on it tonight."

Oh no.

It's five fifty-five and Dustin told me if we aren't sitting at his grandma's dinner table at exactly six sharp she will not be happy with us. She's old-fashioned when it comes to traditions. Dinner

155

has to be religiously on time every night. If you're late your food will be cold and there is no reheating it. He doesn't dare show up late when he can help it.

The farmhouse is stunning inside. We enter through the back door straight into a mudroom. The small room houses a washer, dryer, laundry sink, and shoe rack. We scrub our hands and set our boots on the rack. Spending the majority of the day with the goats and cows in the pasture, we wouldn't dare step foot in the house with them on. The interior is exactly what I'd pictured it would look like, decorated with crisp white walls, warm hardwood floors, antique cuckoo clocks, and scenery paintings. The mudroom leads straight to a dining room with a large oak table, set for four people. The decorating style is inviting and homey.

A woman walks out from the entryway; I assume she's his grandmother. Her long gray hair is tied up on top of her head, a floral apron is wrapped around her waist tied into a neat bow at the front. She beams a wide smile, and I instantly feel at ease in her company. Her presence exudes warmth.

"Gram. This is Violet. Violet, this is Gram," Dustin introduces us.

She wipes her floured hands across the sides of her apron. The dust floats through the air in a cloud. "It is a pleasure to finally meet you, honey. I don't know why we haven't crossed paths before," She pulls me into a tight embrace. The pleasant fragrance of parsley, spices, and a hint of rose fill my nostrils. She pinches my cheeks. "Oh honey you are so pretty."

"Thank you." I blush. "It's nice to meet you Mrs. Rhett." It takes all of my restraint not to rub my sore cheeks. What is it with grandmas and squeezing cheeks? It's painful; they have an iron grip!

"Oh dear, please call me Gram. Anyways, I will be your Gram soon, I hope." She winks at Dustin.

I thought I was blushing before.

I was wrong.

Now my face is a thousand shades of red. I sneak a glance at Dustin. His eyebrows shoot up. He gives me a, *I told you she'd say that* look. I try to stifle a giggle, but cough into my arm instead to cover it up. I never was good at holding in a laugh.

"Please Gram. You're going to scare her away," Dustin chastises her.

"Oh dear, if she's here with you right now there isn't much more I could do. You don't need my help in that department. You would have scared her away already." She shrugs as I snort, covering my face again.

Dustin stares at his grandmother, giving her the stink eye, and grunts a reply, "Way to boost my ego."

"Your ego is big enough for all of us." Gram claps her still-floured hands. "Okay, pleasantries over. Let's eat youngins. I hope you like chicken and dumplings. Because that's what we're having."

My stomach grumbles so loudly. It sounds like thunder booming in the room. I grin sheepishly and look away. Embarrassed by my lack of control when it comes to my appetite. Gram chuckles, seemingly approving of my hunger.

"Where's Grandpa? He's late." Dustin questions her. Dustin pulls out my chair for me and sits to my left. Gram takes a seat across from me.

"He'll be here any second. I sent him into the canning closet to grab us a jar of my homemade applesauce." She checks the watch on her wrist. "He's not late anyway, one more minute until six." I make a mental note to never be late if I'm invited again. He definitely wasn't exaggerating about that.

"What did I miss?" His grandpa walks in, taking a seat next to Gram. "Hi Miss Violet, nice to see you again." He beams a tender smile in my direction.

"Nice to see you again, Mr. Rhett," I say.

"We've been over this. Please call me George. Or better yet, Grandpa. Whatever you prefer."

They are really trying hard to bring me into the family and I can't complain. Being alone for these past two years has been really hard on me. Darcy kept me company for so many years after I lost my parents, always making sure I had a warm meal and time to spend with her each day. She was like a stunning rainbow after a storm. The sunshine after rain, bringing so much warmth and hope into my life. She cared for me when I didn't want to do it for myself anymore. I had no motivation, no will to continue. She pushed me to live my life. To find a small piece of something to look forward to every day.

"Don't let anything steal your joy," was what she'd always say. She was right. Each day got a little bit easier with the grief I held. Then she moved into the retirement home, and it felt like my world was ending all over again. Even though I still visit, it's not the same as living with her.

It feels surreal to be sitting at a dinner table within a family setting. "Dig in," Gram says. "You all need to put some more meat on your bones."

I giggle. Dustin makes eyes at her again and I can tell he's uncomfortable. It looks like he's afraid they may do something to embarrass him. I wish I could tell him there's nothing they could do or say to ruin this dinner. I'm just grateful to be within their company.

We fill our plates with helpings of chicken and dumplings. It's the most delicious meal I have ever eaten. The conversations are mostly between George and Dustin. They've been discussing the work they have planned for tomorrow: checking fences, putting out some hay for the cows, and the prospect of breeding more goats for more milk. A lot of the conversation I have a hard time following. I nod in agreement at all the right times and eat the yummy grub.

"Violet, how are you and Dustin doing in the competitions? Has he been treating you right?" Gram asks me, turning the conversation.

Dustin's hand slightly grazes mine under the table and the connection startles me with a fuzzy feeling, sending electric bolts through my tingling fingers. I say, "They've been—eventful? We fell in a bunch of mud during the treasure hunt. Dustin coaxed a chicken over the finish line to get first place on the first week by complimenting her." I chuckle. "He's been treating me well. I have no complaints. Quite the gentleman saving me from falling multiple times and constantly helping me back up from my clumsiness. You raised him right."

"That's good to hear. You promise to let me know if he gets out of line?"

"Yes ma'am," I say.

"Great, I'll grab the apple pie. George, can you help me with the serving plates?" They both scurry off into the kitchen.

"Thanks for that. I wouldn't have gotten dessert for a month if you would have said one bad thing about me. I know I was a little grumpy with you at first."

"There isn't really anything I can say that's bad." In all honesty he's been nothing but kind to me since we've become friends. It may be true that I thought he was rude when we first met. But today I saw another side of him. A softer one that he hides from the outside world. He's saved me from having a miserable, lonely day spent grieving. He turned it around and now I can say today was the first time since the accident that I have been truly happy on the anniversary. And I think my parents are smiling as they watch me really start to live again.

We finished up dessert, and the pie was just as good as the one Dustin shared with me a week ago. I insisted on helping with the dishes. Dustin scurried off scratching his nose—it's part of the signal we came up with. While his grandpa sits in the living room flicking through the channels, my job is to keep them both occupied for the next thirty or so minutes so that he can set up the antenna on the roof.

This better work. Or else I am never going to live this down.

I'm drying the dishes as Gram scrubs them in the sink. She hands me a plate to dry. I swipe a towel across the smooth surface as we continue to talk.

"Thank you," she says over the running water.

"What for?"

"For bringing the old Dustin back again. I haven't seen him this happy for a long time."

"I didn't do anything." At least I don't think I did.

"You did do something. Even if you don't realize it. There's something different about him. He looks so happy. I don't think I've seen him truly smile like this in years. Every year when we came to see him for the holidays, he was a shell of himself." She hands me another plate. "Dustin used to come here every summer to help on the farm. He would spend every day working on things with George. Building that A-frame he's living in now, bailing hay, learning how to take care of the animals. But as soon as he had to go back home, he would change, his smile would fade. I think this place gives him hope for his future. I think you give him hope. He won't ever admit this, but he secretly loves it here."

The prospect of Dustin staying here warms my heart. I don't want him to leave.

I smile at Gram. "I think so too."

A drilling sound comes from the roof, and I know it's my cue. I really hate to do this, especially to these beautiful ceramic plates. If these were passed down from generations Dustin is going to be sorry, but it was the only way we could distract them from what he was doing.

"What was that?" His grandpa yells from the living room.

I toss the plate when she isn't looking and it shatters into a million pieces. "I'm so sorry!"

This plan is actually genius. With how clumsy I am all of the time, it could be believable that I would break something.

"It's okay honey it's just a plate, no harm done. Let me help you clean that up."

We clean up the pieces and toss them into the trash. I look up to the kitchen window and a cord is swinging back and forth.

We are so caught.

His grandma looks up from the dishes and it's gone. "What's wrong honey? You look like you've seen a ghost."

"No! I just feel really bad about your plate." That's true, I do, but I'm so glad she didn't see that cord.

After cleaning up the mess and finishing up the rest of the dishes Dustin comes strolling in with a grin on his face. "It was a success," he whispers.

"No, it wasn't" I mumble under my breath.

"What was a success?" his grandma asks.

"Oh, I was able to build Violet a wooden sign for her shop in the garage, you probably heard me drilling it."

"That's what that noise was! I thought I was hearing things," his grandpa says over the chatter of the game in the background. Dustin looks at me with pleading eyes.

My lips are sealed.

"That's so sweet of you! Can I see it?"

"Could we show you another time? I'm feeling really tired," I say quickly because I know damn well there isn't a sign anywhere. And once the cat is out of the bag neither of them are going to be happy with Dustin or me.

"Of course, honey, I'll let you two love birds go for the night."

I smile sheepishly as Dustin's gaze meets mine. Gram's beaming with a huge grin as we say goodbye. She even invites me over for dinner whenever I want. The thought almost brings me to tears.

Dustin walks me to his house. Once we are far enough from his grandparents' house I say, "You are ridiculous, you know that right?"

"Why, what did I do?" His eyebrows shoot up.

"Don't look so innocent. You made me break a dish. A plate that has been in your family for generations. It's over a hundred years old. I felt so bad. And she almost saw the cord swinging by the window for five minutes."

"Shit. Was she upset?"

"No, she didn't mind at all. Apparently, she's broken a couple over the years."

"I'm sorry I put you in that position, but now if they never need anything they can call someone."

"That's true. At least one good thing came out of breaking that and giving me heart palpitations." I chuckle. He grins back.

"Can I take you somewhere?" Dustin asks, looking shy for the first time.

"Yes. I don't have anywhere to be," I say.

"I thought you were tired."

"You know I was just trying to save you."

We stop at his house, and he starts up his Grandpa's truck. "Wait here. I'll be right back."

He comes out the door a few minutes later holding a huge bag and throws it into the back with a thud. Dustin climbs in the driver's seat and starts to head to a dirt road at the beginning of the pasture. He gets out to open a large gate and closes it once we pull through.

"Are you going to murder me and shove me in that bag back there?"

"No!" he shouts. "I'm trying to do something nice but failing miserably. Just entertain me?" I nod, pulling my hair out of the ponytail and letting it fall over my shoulders.

He parks the truck in the middle of the field. A picturesque sky meets the green grass. Trees scatter around like little dots in the distance. The hillside slopes around the valley we are parked in. There aren't any buildings or lights in sight.

He unzips the bag and pulls out two huge comforters and pillows and sets them up in the back of the truck. He pulls out two old-fashioned battery powered lanterns, arranging everything up nice and cozy for us to lay down in. I watch him in awe.

No one has ever done anything like this for me. I feel like I'm living a scene out of a movie.

We lay down next to each other on our backs and stare at the sky. It's unlike anything I've ever dreamt of. Pastel pinks, light blues, and white wisps paint it like a canvas. Each stroke is intentional. Making for the most jaw-dropping sunset. The peaceful sounds of birds singing and cows mooing echo in the distance. It's as if the sound is pure nature. My breath hitches in awe. The view from town is similar, but nothing compares to the sight of nothing else but us. I rack my brain for the right words to describe it. But nothing comes to mind, so I settle with the one thing I can think of: "This is—wow—beautiful."

"I used to think that too, but things have changed," he says, staring up at the sky.

"What changed?" I wonder out loud.

"You." He turns his head to the side to look at me. "*You* are more beautiful than the sunset. More so than all of the stars in the sky." I look into his blue eyes; they are filled with sincerity. It's then I believe his words. It shocks me to my core. He stares at my lips and back into my heady gaze. It's just like the time we lay in the mud. But this time there isn't cold rain pelting us, or mud caked all over me. This time I know what I want.

I press my lips against his hesitantly. Bursts of fireworks explode in my stomach at the connection. At first, the mere touch is hesitant and gentle. Instantly soft yet captivating. It sends a shiver down my spine. All thoughts are a blur. He traces his fingers over my jaw and strands of unruly hair out of my closed eyes. I smile against his touch. Dustin's lips are inviting, smooth, mesmerizing. I want to savor this moment forever. I know that it won't ever be enough. Inevitably one of us will have to break away. The trees, sky, and soon reality too fade into the background as the kiss deepens. I never knew it could feel like this. I've only kissed a few other guys, but nothing ever felt this exceptional.

I put my fingers through his hair and with my other hand I hold his cheek, feeling the stubble on his face. It's scratchy against my touch. I let go suddenly because I have to get something off my chest.

"Are we still friends? Because friends don't normally kiss," I say in all seriousness. Unless they're friends with benefits. But I don't want us to be like that.

"Yes, we'll always be friends, but that's what I wanted to talk to you about."

My heart drops to my stomach.

Does he want to end this so-called friendship and be done with me? Have I scared him off? Did I do something wrong?

The doubts run through my mind. I've ruined so many things in my life before. I'm not ready to lose this one good thing that's just within my grasp.

Dustin tilts my head up and his gaze meets mine. "I don't want to be *just* anything anymore. We were just enemies. Maybe we could have been considered rivals at one point. Who am I kidding—we were never enemies. We were just acquaintances, just friends. I want more, so much more."

My eyes fill with unshed tears. "So what do you want to be?"

"Well, you could start off with being my girlfriend."

My heart races a mile a minute. Ready to beat directly out of my chest. I have never felt this way about a man before. Passion filled visceral feelings. It's terrifying and exhilarating at the same time. My decision is clear. "I'd love that."

He hugs me tighter as the sky slowly transitions from indigo to black. The stars sparsely spread across the darkness, peeking out from the pitch-black sky. A chill fills the air, but I'm not cold. I feel so warm and safe in his arms. I don't ever want to leave his embrace.

Chapter 27

VIOLET

It's been one day, technically one night, since Dustin and I have become more than friends. They've already dubbed us the new "*it*" couple in town. Plastered all over the town's social media page, with one long article, written by none other than the Gossip Mill. They work fast because it was published at four in the morning. The post is filled with quotes from the town folks on our sightings. One from Sophia, co-owner of The Cozy Cabin Inn, confirming a sighting of us kissing goodbye in front of my shop last night. Then it all gets worse because I didn't even get a chance to tell Olive yet. I wanted to break the news in person. But no, I couldn't do it on my own; they had to beat me to it. Dustin told his Gram last night, she told her best friend Jane, and Jane told Bobbie. You could guess what happened from there.

Dustin sent me an apologetic text and I know he didn't mean to announce it to the whole town overnight, so I just shrugged it off. I wouldn't mind if only I had sent Olive some kind of text last night to tell her. She's going to be so mad at me.

I flip the open sign on the front door. It's exactly seven and there are already customers lined up. They're here for one reason, and one reason only. To find out information.

At least I think so.

"Good morning everyone!" I greet the ladies standing at the door. "Come on in and get out of the rain." They all file in, closing their umbrellas and hanging their coats on the coat rack next to the door. The ladies all browse flowers and plants. Which shocks me. This is more business than I have ever had this early in the morning. I thought they would all hound me for the details of how we ended up together, but they are looking for things to purchase. A few of the townies purchase bouquets, others choose house plants. A few congratulate me on my relationship. Once the crowd is gone, I sigh in relief as I sit on the couch.

Olive comes rushing in the door with a purpose. Her raincoat flaps in the wind along with the swinging door. She shrugs her coat on the hanger and beelines straight to me.

Oh no.

"I am so happy for you!" Olive squeals as she hops onto the couch. Her arms pull me into a squeezing hug.

What? This is not what I expected at all. I was preparing for the worst.

"You're not mad that I didn't tell you?"

"Of course not! I know how the gossip mill works. You would have told me if you had the chance." She lets me go and leans back on the couch.

"Who's watching the coffee shop?" I wonder how she's able to be here during opening hours. It's a peak business hour for coffee. Otherwise, the townies turn into zombies without their caffeine fix.

"Mason was grabbing coffee and offered to cover for a few while I talked to you. I was telling him all about you and Dustin. And how badly I wanted to talk to you in person about it," she stammers, fidgeting with the keys in her hand.

"Oh Mason? What's going on there?"

"We're just friends. You know this. Anyway, I'm here to talk about *you,* not me." She brushes some of her red hair onto her back. "Please let me say my piece and then I have to get back. I couldn't wait until this afternoon to say it."

When I don't stop her, she continues, "I knew it. I knew something was going on between you two. You had a thing for him all along, whether you wanted to admit it or not. I'm so happy for you. After your last relationship I thought you would never let someone in again. I'm so glad I was wrong. You deserve to be happy. And you need to let go of everything that you blame yourself for. Jackson cheating on you was not your fault. Your parents' accident was not your fault. Please don't forget that." Tears form in the corner of her eyes.

"Thank you. I don't know what I would do without you."

"I don't know what I would do without you either. But I need to go, before the coffee is all burnt and I lose customers. Plus, we will both be a crying mess if I stay."

Now I'm alone in my thoughts repeating what she just said: *You deserve to be happy.* She's right. I need to stop self-sabotaging.

Chapter 28

VIOLET

We thought Bobbie's Freeze would be a good treat after spending hours practicing for the final competition, a three-legged race, with no luck. After countless falls my body couldn't take anymore. So, we called it a day and chose to wing it tomorrow.

The shop feels instantly cool when stepping inside. The walls are decorated with painted brick, designed to look like blocks of ice. We order our ice cream and sit at a table in front of the large glass window. Dustin sits across from me with a sundae. He takes a huge bite—a spoonful of vanilla with hot fudge, sprinkles, and chopped nuts. Then he asks, "Who decided this three-legged race was a good idea?"

That is a question I've pondered myself many times. Especially with the older small business owners. It's a recipe for disaster. Some teams will sub someone out for this challenge so that no one gets hurt—they allow it because of disasters in previous years.

"Twenty years ago someone on the founders of this competition decided it was a great idea. No one has changed the last competition since then." Which I think is ridiculous, nonetheless. "And the worst part is you're so much taller than me. Making this even more challenging than teams with people that are close in height." I grab a spoon full of mint chocolate chip ice cream and the chill from it is refreshing against the beads of sweat trailing down my back.

"How did you do in this one last year?" he says between bites.

"Not well. We placed last." My shoulders shake in laughter. "Tripped and fell straight out of the start line. Dan and I struggled to get back up for a couple of minutes. By the time we did, everyone was already at the halfway mark. And there was no coming back."

"Well that just means we have to keep practicing. Tomorrow before the race we can practice a couple runs. I have time."

"That works for me." I take the last bite of my ice cream pointing at the empty container. "This right here is the key to my heart."

"So, all I had to do was get you some toothpaste flavored ice cream and you would have fallen for me."

I blink my eyes shyly looking up with a deviant smile. "Yes. But it doesn't taste like toothpaste, it's delicious."

"You can't convince me otherwise." His lips lift slightly in the corner. He gets up from his chair and grabs our bowls to throw them out. He kisses me quickly on the lips. My cheeks flush. I'm still not used to being in a relationship. But it's a pleasant surprise.

I look over at the counter, noticing Bobbie and one of the younger workers swooning. They snicker to each other and fan themselves with menus. When they catch my gaze, their eyes quickly dart away. They both hastily duck under the counter. Menus fly through the air and the sound of giggling reverberates over the tune of a Patsy Cline song.

I can't help but grin at the sight. The best thing about a small town is the fact that everyone knows each other. Well, most of the time I love that. Unless you want privacy, then it's no fun, because you can never hide anything. The news of our new relationship will soon blow over when the events commence tomorrow. New articles will be written on their social page, and we'll be old news.

I hope so, for my sanity.

"Are you ready?" He outstretches his hand.

"Yes, let's go." I place mine in his, and the connection sends tingles through my fingers. I wonder if he feels the same thing when we touch. I've never had this kind of reaction to someone else before.

We walk across the sidewalk as the sun is setting. The glow from the sky illuminates his face. The dimples in the corner of his cheeks are prominent.

"Did you ever find out if the antenna worked? Is their cell service any better?"

"I honestly forgot. Let's find out." He dials his grandpa and puts it on speaker.

"Hello?"

"Hello Dustin."

"I just wanted to let you know I grabbed you and Gram some ice cream from town and I'm bringing it over now."

"You didn't have to call to tell me that, you could have just brought it over. You kids and having to sit by the phone constantly."

I giggle in the background, trying to muffle my laugh to no eval.

"What's so funny?"

"Nothing! Got to go." Dustin hangs up and bursts into laughter. "Our mission was successful."

"I still can't believe you made me break one of her fine china plates."

"Sacrifices were made."

"Are you ready to pay up your end of the bargain?"

"Hit me with it."

Chapter 29

DUSTIN

"This is what you needed my help with?" I say.

"Yes! I need to find out who H is. It's killing me and she won't tell me!" Violet says.

"Who is H?"

"That's what I'm trying to figure out!"

"Let's go across the street and ask her."

"You don't think I already tried that?"

"Well, I don't know."

"It didn't work, but we can try again, let's go."

"You're a hoot!" Darcy says while looking in my direction.

"Don't say that to him; it will go to his head and make his ego bigger than it already is." Violet scoffs.

"Oh dear, he is, don't deny what we both already know."

"Yes dear. I am a hoot," I say to Violet. She just grumbles something under her breath.

"So, we came to find out who H is. Can you tell us?" Violet asks with pleading eyes.

"He's just a friend, no one special."

"You are such a liar! I thought we made a deal once I told you about Dustin, you would tell me about your secret love."

"I said maybe, not yes."

"Oh, come on please tell us. I'm dying to know."

"If you want, I'll tell you a story about when I was younger."

"Please tell us," Violet says.

"When I was freshly graduated and twenty, I was so fed up with this small town that I left. I thought that I needed to travel the world to experience life. I hitchhiked to Woodstock all by myself, I met a few friends along the way. The experience was out of this world. It was so peaceful, full of music, friends, and love. The weather wasn't ideal though. Now remember, this was in the seventies when everyone had long hair, fringe everything, tie-dye. You should have seen me—I was a picture of nostalgia. I never saw so many people in one place in my life. I met H there. And that's all you're getting!"

"Oh come on! Who is he?" Violet begs, desperation in her tone.

"Look what time it is." She taps a non-existent watch on her arm. "It's time for dinner. I'll have to tell you next time." She averts her gaze to the nurse strolling in the door with a dinner tray.

"I told you she wouldn't give it up." Violet drops her shoulders. "But at least it was a good day, and she remembered who I was. Also, we did get another clue at least."

"We tried, but now we will have to go straight to the source."

"That's what I was dreading."

Chapter 30

Violet

A gaggle of townies and tourists crowd the park. Children are lining up behind the row of slides, giggling as they swoosh down on potato sacks. I don't think I've ever seen this many people in one place here before. Some are seated in fold-up lawn chairs lining the open field, scattered around chatting. The same lines painted for the chicken race were given a fresh coat. Thankfully, the rain has quit long enough for the grass to dry up so that we aren't racing in mud.

I feel the grass beneath my feet. The subtle smell of barbeque swifts into my nose out of a tent where Rooster's Bar is catering. It's a refreshing sight to see everyone come together for the day. And it puts a smile on my face.

At the last competition every year they set up a raffle for baskets. Every business creates a basket full of a few things. I donated plants, a gift card, some flowers, and a few vouchers for free flower arrangements. Dustin made a basket full of soap, candles, lip balms all made from the goat's milk. Even a few coupons for cheese to spend at the Valley Harvest. Now that he was able to get some cheese stocked there. This raffle really helps to raise money for the businesses, and it's a fun way to have activities for everyone who shows up.

"Hey!" I greet Olive, Mason, and Chloe.

"Hey girl!" Olive smiles. "Mason was just telling us all about the chicks that just hatched."

"No way! What kind of chickens did you get this time?"

"Five Salmon Faverolles."

"What do they look like?" I ask.

"Their feathers are white and brown and they lay brown eggs. They are also cold hardy so they will lay eggs in the winter."

"When did you get them?" Chloe pipes in.

"Yesterday. They were delivered to the post office from a hatchery in Ohio. Laura was so excited, she spent the morning with them while she worked. Then I picked them up around noon."

"They deliver them in the mail?" Chloe asks.

"Yep. If you want, you can come see them. I have them separated in the chicken coop. Olive spent hours with them yesterday, but I'm sure she would love to introduce you both to them." He grins at her. Her face flushes crimson.

I shoot Olive a knowing stare.

Mason and Olive have been friends forever. I can tell they have chemistry, but I don't think Olive has ever noticed it. I try to stay out of her love life the best I can. But when she needs advice I am always there for her, just like she always has been for me.

"Ahh," I yelp when I feel strong hands wrap around my waist to pull me backward.

"It's just me Vivi," Dustin's husky voice murmurs in my ear. And he pulls me into the front of his chest. A pleasant woodsy smell penetrates my nose, pine and a touch of sandalwood. I melt in his embrace.

"You two are so adorable." Olive sighs. I don't miss the longing glance Mason gives her.

"There's Constance holding her signature microphone, I guess she traded it for the megaphone," Chloe chimes in.

"I gotta go! I have to talk to her." I pull Dustin along because we are in this one together. He owes me after all.

"It's so nice to see you two together." Constance smiles.

"Thanks. We have a couple questions for you if you have the time," Dustin says.

"Sure, I have a few minutes to spare before the competition starts."

"Do you know if Darcy was ever friends with anyone whose name started with H in town? I know there's Henry from the Valley Harvest and Harvey from Fix-Its. They are both about her age."

"Let me think." She scratches her head in concentration. "I do remember them hanging out all of the time when they were younger. That's right. They met at Woodstock. Henry always tells the story when I come around. They became good friends, and he followed her back to town and started working at the Food Save before he purchased it. Then he named it The Valley Harvest and the rest is history. Sometimes I see Henry walking into the retirement home. I was wondering who he was visiting. Now it makes sense. I can ask around for you. What do you need to know?"

"No, no. That's exactly what I was looking for, thank you. You've been a great help." I don't want to ask too many questions. Darcy would not be happy about the story being posted on the social media page.

As we walk away I whisper to Dustin, "So it was Henry all along. I'm talking to him after this is over."

"We better line up. Looks like Constance is getting her microphone ready."

We all make our way to the red line. Each team's color coordinated ropes are sitting along the start line.

"Get ready everyone, the final competition of the small business games starts in a few minutes. This will be a three-legged race. I'm sorry to have to say this but here are the rules. Rule number one, no shoving any competitors or you are disqualified. Rule number two, your bands must all be snug around your legs. Do not loosen them. Rule number three, there are no other rules. The first group to cross the finish line wins the entire thing! Ready? Three, two, one, go!"

On go everyone takes off in a flash. I try my best to do everything we practiced. Starting with counting in my head one, two, three, four. The rhythm helps me focus to keep our synchronization. If I don't break this method, I won't trip us both up. But there are others that are already way ahead. Dustin is so tall compared to me so we're at a huge disadvantage. The other two teams, Chelsea and Laura, and Annie and Olive, are both similar in height. So, they have a better chance of winning this one.

I also can't help but get distracted by the crowd of people surrounding us.

My leg is so tight against his, constrained by the strap wrapped at my calf. Our pace is steady, just like we practiced. And we are starting to catch up. As we pass team green, I start to feel hope. Everyone is shouting different things. "Go team purple! Go team orange! Go team green!" All of the chaos makes me forget to count. My left foot steps at the wrong time, and we both go flying.

He lets out a loud harumph. The wind gets knocked out of my lungs on the impact. Dustin starts chuckling. It's contagious because I start giggling as well. We lie on the ground laughing. All while the crowd is shrieking around us. But I don't notice anything else. These games were made so that the town could fundraise to keep all of the small shops in town in business. It is supposed to bring everyone together, to have fun. We don't need to win;

it wouldn't make much of a difference either way. I've gained so much from being paired with Dustin, and I would never take any of that back. Sure, he may have been insufferable at first. Okay, I was also insufferable. But once we got to know each other, we clicked. I can now say I am so glad we were paired together.

"Our winners are team green! Annie and Olive! Let's hear it for them!" Constance bellows. The gaggles of people shout in triumph for a few minutes until they quiet down. "Alright, congrats to you two! The Olive bean and Annie's Diner will both receive plaques for their store windows this year. Since it is our anniversary you both get a two-night stay at the Thornwood cabins, all expenses paid. This can be redeemed whenever you like, and you each will get your own cabin. Also, free haircuts for a year at the Chop shop for you both!"

"Damn! I can't believe we missed out on free haircuts. I could have really used that." Dustin messes his hair up, proving his point. "Too bad we lost. If you weren't so clumsy we might have had a chance."

"I'm clumsy over you."

"I wouldn't have it any other way." Dustin's confession makes me feel all warm and fuzzy inside. My lips curve into a small smile, but I drop it when I see Chelsea running back towards town with tears in her eyes.

"I have to go, I'll text you." I peck Dustin quickly on the lips and book it towards her quickly retreating form. No one notices our departure, they are all too engrossed in the activities.

I catch up to her at the back entrance to The Chop Shop. I gasp trying to suck in air.

I really need to get in better shape. All of this pizza and pepperoni rolls are starting to weigh me down. "Chelsea, wait!" She turns around to look at me. Her eyes are puffy and cheeks are tear stained.

"What do you want? Did you follow me to rub the loss in my face? Because there's no point, you can forget it. I'm a failure."

"No, I'm not here to rub anything in. I wanted to make sure you were okay." I pull her into a hug. After a while she puts her arms around me. I let her cry until her sobs calm.

She pulls away and we both sit down on a park bench. "Why do you care if I'm okay? After everything I did to you."

"Because you're hurting, and you need someone there for you. Everyone makes mistakes. I couldn't care less about the past right now. For a while I wanted to beat you in the competitions because of everything that was done to Olive and I. But that wasn't truly your fault. It can all be blamed on Jackson and Chad." Her silence is deafening. The laughter and chatter from the park is a low murmur in the distance.

She speaks up after a few minutes. "I try so hard with the competitions because of my mom. Constance is always worried about everyone else, the town, the gossip. She never seems to notice her own daughter. I thought that if I won, she would finally notice me. It worked for a few years, but when I lost today I broke down. To make things worse Chad broke up with me; turns out he just wanted to make Olive jealous. I pushed all of my friends away trying to get my mom to notice me. How pathetic am I?"

"You're not pathetic. His name is Chad, he is a *Chad*. He's the pathetic one." She laughs. "And your mom loves you, but she is always worried about everything going on. You should try and talk to her about it. I'm sure she doesn't even know what she's doing. Also, we can be friends."

"I will try. Thank you, Violet. You'd really be my friend?"

"Of course I would. But no more trying to steal boyfriends. That goes against friend code."

"Okay." Her voice is hesitant but underlined with hope.

"Pinky swear it."

"Pinky swear." She grabs my finger, and we swear on our new friendship.

Chapter 31

DUSTIN

"Hey Farmer Dustin! It's been ages. You look the part now," Nolan yells at me from the baked goods stand. He approaches me with a whoopie pie in one hand and a coffee in the other.

I clap him on the back. "It's good to see you man. How'd the trip here treat you?"

"Once I got out of New York—the trip was—a breeze," he says in between bites of whoopie pie. "Holy shit these are to die for. Give me a hundred more to take home."

"You can buy the whole lot. They have a good 200 more on the table."

"I think I might."

"So did you just come here to watch me lose miserably and rub it in my face."

"Yes and no. While it gives me great pleasure to see you fall on your ass, I have an ulterior motive."

I assumed as much; he never does something without a plan. Most of the time it involves anything business related. The man puts his career above everything, including himself.

Something I used to do too.

"I'm starting my own company. I'm leaving the firm. And I want you to be a partner."

"Are you serious? Why me?"

"I need someone with financial and accounting experience. Someone I trust. We worked together, I know how seriously you take your job. You have years on your belt, and you're in the perfect position where you have nothing holding you back anymore."

"What kind of firm are you starting?"

"One that solely focuses on helping small businesses. I haven't come up with a name for it yet. I want to help them with multiple services: bookkeeping, payroll, taxes, advisory. The focus will be on building connections. Working closely with them, so that I can help the community, not large corporations. I want to make a difference. Seeing shops struggle and you moving here gave me the inspiration I needed."

"I'll have to think about it, but I really appreciate the offer."

"No problem, you deserve it. I have to get back to the city, but I wanted to ask you in person. Now I gotta grab some whoopie pies to go. Nice seeing you brother."

You have nothing holding you back anymore. His words ring through my mind. Is that true? I didn't when I first moved back, but now? I have a lot holding me back. The farm, the town, Violet, my grandparents. Everything in me is screaming to stay, but should I give up the career I worked to achieve? On the other hand, should I give up my happiness for a successful career? I think I know the answer to that one.

But I still have to think about it. This is a once in a lifetime opportunity.

Chapter 32

VIOLET

"It's been an insane four weeks."

"You're telling me! I'm so tired." Olive shoves a handful of snacks into her mouth.

A girls' night has been long overdue. A movie night is infinitely better. We're watching *White Chicks* and lounging on my couch eating snacks. Loads of snacks. Funyuns, chocolate covered pretzels, chocolate bunnies (since The Valley Harvest is selling them already in preparation for Easter), Cheetos, Doritos. Every unhealthy snack is on the table. I have no regrets. Tomorrow I might, but not tonight. "You could call this a girl dinner."

"What's a girl dinner?" I say in between bites of a chocolate bunny.

"Only a dinner made up of a bunch of random things that have no rhyme or reason to go together. Just a bunch of snacks that make a meal."

"So what's a boy dinner?"

"No clue, probably something boring." We both shake with laughter.

I could have snacks every night instead of a regular meal. Snacks are the key to my heart and now I guess a *girl dinner* is too. "Do you ever feel bad for biting their little chocolate bunny heads off? I kind of feel guilty when eating them."

"No." Olive takes one massive bite into the bunny's head, crunching on it with no care in the world. She holds up her headless chocolate bunny in the air like a trophy.

"I'm appalled. I feel threatened by your aggressive behavior towards the poor little bunnies." I slide all of the bunnies back into their container and beeline it to the kitchen.

"No! Wait! Don't leave with them! I need more chocolate," Olive yells. I book it, running as fast as I can. She jumps, flying through the air and tackles me John Cena style. I hit the ground with a thud. She pins me to the carpet in her crushing grip. I flail underneath her grasp trying to get free with no avail. "Olive Watson, the winner of today's match!" She takes the chocolate out of my hands, opens the container and bites the head off another bunny.

"You monster!" I yell.

Yes, this is what I meant about not wanting to be on her bad side. I should have never tried to hide the bunnies.

"We're missing the best part of the movie!" She rushes back over to the couch holding her container of bunnies.

"We've watched it a thousand times." I shrug nonchalantly.

"Your point."

"Point is if we miss a few minutes, I'm sure we can piece back what we missed from our memory, or you could just rewind it."

Olive rewinds the movie so that we can have the full experience. We spend the next hour devouring snacks until we both are in a food coma.

"How are you and Dustin?" Olive breaks the silence.

"I'm really happy with him, but I'm so afraid he will run for the hills when he knows the truth," I admit freely. Knowing she will have advice for me.

"You're kidding right?"

"No?"

"That drunk driver hitting your parents' car wasn't your fault. You know it, I know it, Darcy knows it. He won't leave you for something that you had nothing to do with. Trust me."

"I do." I know I've harped on this before, but she's right. I need to learn to stop blaming myself for something that wasn't my fault. I can't help but feel like he might look at me differently, though.

"Good, then don't worry about it, and tell him when the time feels right."

"I really like him. It might even be more than like. Is it too soon for that? We've only known each other for over a month."

"When you find the one there's no time limit constraining you on how fast or slow you fall. It just happens without you even realizing it."

"When did you become so wise?"

"After dealing with Chad for too long, I've learned a few things about Mr. *not* right."

Chapter 33

VIOLET

"You look—breathtakingly beautiful." Dustin surveys my outfit up and down in appreciation. I blush hardcore, my whole face is warm. I'm not used to compliments and it makes my heart skip a beat.

I will admit I spent an hour getting ready for our date. That is unusual for me. I added some mascara for a touch of a done up look. I curled my hair and fluffed up my bangs the best I could. I decided on a pair of blue jeans and a brown flare sleeved, scalloped trimmed shirt. I even broke out a pair of western platform boots I had sitting in the back of my closet. It's a little out of my comfort zone, but I thought I would try something different.

"Thank you. You clean up nice too." I smile shyly, taking in his blue flannel shirt and jeans. He paired his outfit with a clean pair of leather boots.

Dustin and I are going on our first *actual* date to Annie's. It's nothing outrageously fancy, but it's perfect for the both of us. I've been looking forward to this all week.

"Ladies first," Dustin drawls, holding the door open for me and letting me go in the restaurant first like the true gentleman he is. We take our seats and he pulls out a chair for me. We order our drinks. A sprite for me and a root beer for him. He insisted on driving, so he didn't want to order alcohol.

"So what's good here?"

"Everything. But if you want the secret menu, I'll share it with you."

"What's on the secret menu?"

"I don't know about you, but I love a good thanksgiving plate in the spring. You can order turkey, stuffing, mashed potatoes, gravy, and the works. All you have to tell the waitress is, 'the fixin's meal.' She'll know what that means."

"I'm getting that."

"Me too." I pause to give the waitress our order and she spins away to the back.

"Do you ever want to travel anywhere? If you had the chance to go anywhere in the world, where would you want to go?

"I always wanted to go to Alaska. I love the snow and the cold. You can always bundle up more layers, but you can't take them off. Well, you can if you're into indecent exposure in public," I joke. "Seriously though, looking at pictures of the northern lights, mountains, stretches of nothing but wildlife. I think it would be a dream to go there one day. What about you?"

"I never had a desire to travel anywhere, but after hearing you talk about Alaska like that, seeing the light in your eyes when you think of going there...I know that's where I would want to go. With you of course."

I grab his hand across the table, intertwining my fingers with his. The heat in his stare has me feeling something more than like. But is it love?

"That would be nice."

"So you never really came to town when you visited as a child?"

"No, only on occasions. My grandparents would take me to Jacks Bar, before it was renamed to Roosters. Every establishment in town is renamed multiple times. I think the new names give them all character." He runs his thumb across my hand. "They would sneak me in to watch The Heartbreakers play. It was the highlight of my stay."

"No way! I used to go with Darcy. I bet we even crossed paths at some time. I'm sure of it."

"We had to have. I used to hang out with Mason all the time, since his parents owned the bar."

"I used to sit with Mason and Olive and watch them play. We may have even sat at the same table."

"It's a small world."

"More like a small town. You're bound to cross paths."

"You're right about that. I think I know everyone now."

We clean our plates, devouring all of the food, laughing and conversing over the next hour. We learn so much more about each other. I don't know what it is about a restaurant environment, but it makes me feel like I can share anything in the world with him. We both end up refusing dessert after being too full to even fit another bite.

"That was really nice." He takes my hand in his as we walk down the sidewalk towards my shop.

"We should do it again sometime."

"I think I can arrange that." His smirk is so devastatingly handsome.

By the time we reach the front door of my shop he sweeps me off my feet with a heart-melting kiss. As our lips brush, my insides melt into a puddle. Every time we are together my walls come down a bit more and I just want to tell him everything. I want this to last, but I don't want to ruin the moment.

Chapter 34

DUSTIN

One month later

It's been a crazy whirlwind of a month. I still haven't made any decisions on whether I will stay or take up Nolan's offer. I've been so busy with work on the farm. It's been constantly storming and raining. We've had to do a lot of fence mending with the strong winds. Calving season has been in full swing so it's a constant battle.

Then Violet and I's relationship has been in full swing. We've gone on dates. We normally just eat at Gram's or go out to the diner. I've spent every waking moment of free time with her. I don't even know how I functioned before without her. And I spend every moment without her, thinking about her.

DUSTIN

Do you want to come over to my place for dinner tonight and have movie marathons?

VIOLET

I would love that. You cook?

DUSTIN

Yes, but I'm not the best cook. Gram can cook us something special.

VIOLET

At least you're honest. See you around 6.

"I'm here!"

"It's one fifteen, you're too late for lunch. It's cold."

"Please Gram I'm starving! I had to feed the goats. They were acting out of control. I woke up late, after staying up last night helping a cow with a breech birth, can you blame me?"

"Should have been up before the rooster's crow." My grandfather yells from the living room. I roll my eyes.

"Ignore him, I will heat you up a plate because you are my favorite grandson." I'm her only grandson, but I guess I'll take the compliment.

"Thank you! I also need a small favor."

She puts her hands on her hips. A dusting of flour fills the air from the motion. She's constantly covered in it. That's how you know her food is the best. Everything is made with her hands. "How do I know it's not going to be a small one?"

"Because you know me better than myself."

"What is it?"

"Could you make fried chicken with macaroni and cheese? They're one of Violet's favorites and she's coming over to my place for dinner tonight. You know I can't cook something to save my life unless it's breakfast food."

"One condition."

"And that is?" My eyes narrow.

"You and I will make it together."

That I can work with. "Deal."

"Deal," she repeats and shakes my hand.

After hours spent in the kitchen, we finally have the macaroni and cheese in the oven. And all of the chicken is done. I taste tested one too many pieces of chicken and got the *look*. The one that will earn me a backhand to the head if I ate any more. Begrudgingly, I stopped taste testing after that. I'm not in the mood for a headache.

"I got a job offer," I blurt unexpectedly as we lean against the kitchen counter sipping on hot chocolate.

I hadn't meant to say anything, but I guess it's been on my mind ever since Nolan spoke to me a couple weeks ago. I am torn between staying and going, leaning less towards the latter. I wanted a few months' trial at the farm and that is about up.

"I'm so proud of you. When do you leave?"

"What?" I just about spit out the hot chocolate coating my throat. "Are you that eager for me to get out of your hair? I didn't think I was that much of a nuisance."

"No! That's not what I meant. I want whatever is best for you. It has to be something you decide on your own. If you want this farm, it's yours, but if you want to pursue a life in the city as an accountant or whatever you choose to do, then I'm happy for you. I want you to live *your* dream. Do whatever makes *you* happy. Don't settle on the farm because you want to make your grandfather happy. I don't care what the old geezer thinks about it. He's stubborn, but he'll forgive you in time. He loves you. And I do too."

"You're making me tear up Gram."

She pulls me in a flour-dusted embrace. We're both covered this time. I wouldn't want it any other way. Cooking with my grandmother is exactly where I want to be. I will never be able to trade this moment for anything else.

I can't leave now, I realize. I love it here.

Chapter 35

VIOLET

"What do I do?"

"What do you mean? What do you do?"

"I think he wants me to stay the night. Should I pack a bag?" I peel open a drawer in my dresser to look for some clothes to wear for dinner.

"I'll tell you what you shouldn't do," Olive says while lounging on my bed petting my cat.

"What's that?" I ask as I grab my pajamas and stuff them in a bag.

"Wear those chicken pajamas."

"Why not? I think they're cute."

"Because you will never get laid wearing those."

"And who says I'm trying to get laid?"

"You're just going to sleep then?"

"I don't know what's going to happen, but I'm bringing the chicken pajamas they're my favorite and they're comfortable."

"You're infuriating."

"But you love me."

"Mhmm."

"Seriously, what do I do if it does come to that?"

"That's up to you. Don't go there if you aren't ready, but if you are, don't stop yourself. Try not to compare your previous relationships to this one and give him the chance he deserves."

"You always know the right thing to say."

"That's because I'm always right."

I roll my eyes.

Three hours later my legs are completely silky smooth, Olive insisted I prepare somewhat just in case. I'm wearing my best jeans and a T-shirt. Bag in hand also *just in case*—her words not mine. However, I ended up bringing the chicken pajamas. She couldn't change my mind. I'm so nervous, my palms are clammy and my heart is pounding so loud I swear it's going to beat right out of my chest.

Why is this so scary?

I know why. It's scary because I like him so much. I don't want to mess things up. After standing at his door for a good five minutes, I work up the courage to knock on it.

"Come in!" Dustin shouts from inside.

It's now or never.

I give myself a pep talk and decide to take the risk. "What's that delicious smell?" It wafts through the open door as I step in. Cheese, garlic, and something I can't pinpoint makes my stomach grumble.

"Mac and Cheese, your favorite."

"You remembered?" I can't believe he remembered that.

"Of course I did, now come eat, I'm starving. I've been slaving over my grandmother's stove for hours."

"You're lying!"

"I guess you'll never know." He chuckles.

Sardine runs up to me at a fast pace and I haul him into my arms. "You are the cutest little guy ever! I missed you!" He purrs in my ear as he nuzzles against me.

"Are you coming, or are you only here for my cat?"

"I guess I'll eat with you." I giggle while placing Sardine back on the ground. I grab a toy mouse from my bag and throw it for him, making a mental note to buy him more toys just because he deserves it.

We dig into our plates of macaroni and cheese with fried chicken. After I learned he and his grandmother made this food I was elated. They're going to make me gain so much weight. Their food is out of this world. I've spent the past few weeks gorging on soup, casseroles, and bread. I've gained at least five pounds already. Still, I devour one helping of food and plate another.

"Are you ever thinking about going back to New York? Or is farm life growing on you?"

"To be honest, Nolan approached me at the last competition and offered me a partnership. He wants to start his own company and make me a partner—"

I cut him off, "Wow, that's huge news! An amazing opportunity. Are you going to take it?"

"I told him I would think about it."

Oh.

My heart drops. He can't move back to New York! Not after everything. Well, he can, but I don't want him to. It's shocking to me how much I like him already. I *really* like him. If he leaves now, I'm going to be devastated. I didn't want to feel anything towards anyone again. At least romantically. I was happy to have another friend in my life. But I started feeling more anyway, without even trying.

"I thought about it over the past few weeks. I was unsure until today. I got some much needed advice from my Gram. She always knows the right thing to say. Anyways, I called and turned down the offer."

"Really? Why would you turn it down?" I can't help but feel relief, but it's a huge opportunity. Offers like this one don't come by very often. I wouldn't want him giving up his dreams because of me. I want him to be happy. And if that's in NYC, who am I to strip him of what he wants in life?

"I realized that I belong here. The small-town pace of life is where I feel comfortable. Everything in the city life was too fast paced. I was miserable at my office job. Every day I woke up dreading having to go to work and pretend like I was someone completely different. When I wake up in the morning here I do it with a smile on my face. Even at five in the morning, how sick is that? I can take care of my grandparents if I stay here. Tend to the land just like my grandfather. Help provide food for the community. Cook with my grandmother and learn all of her secret recipes passed down from generations. Also, I met this girl I kind of like."

"Who's this girl? Can I meet her?"

"It's you, silly."

I can't even try to hide my smile now.

Chapter 36

VIOLET

"Are those chickens on your pants?"

"Yes, indeed they are."

"I love them. Come here." I jump onto his couch and curl into his outstretched arms. The nerves I felt before are long gone. I don't know why I got worked up. It was for no reason at all.

"Really? Olive told me I should wear something else. She was so mad at me for bringing these," I say, snuggling against him.

"I wouldn't want you to be anything other than yourself. They suit you perfectly." He kisses me softly on my cheek. "I want every little piece of you. Messy hair, crazy chicken T-shirts, chicken pajamas, camo crocs and all."

"Is that true?"

"You are beautiful darling."

He clicks on the television, and we watch *Shrek 1*, my all-time favorite movie. I snuggle against him, feeling the steady rise and fall of his chest. Sardine curls up next to me. A huge quilt drapes over top of us all, bundling us in a warm cocoon. I could get used to this.

Once the movie ends the screen flashes the credits and I snuggle closer. Dustin brushes a strand of hair behind my ear, and it tingles against my skin. I never get tired of the feeling of his touch. He leans down and crashes his lips against mine.

Every time our lips meet, everything around me blurs in comparison. I used to wonder if he felt the magnetic pull between us when we touched. Now I know for certain that he does. The passion behind every touch is heady. And I want more. I need more this time.

"Dustin." My voice comes out scratchy.

"Violet." His breathy voice answers.

"Please take me to bed."

"Are you sure?" I nod, unable to form any coherent sentences. He tosses me over his shoulder in one swift motion. I giggle the whole way up the stairs as I dangle, watching each step disappear through my fallen hair. He sets me down slowly on my feet and we stare at each other in the dim light of his bedroom. Stars flicker above us in the skylight windows, cascading a passionate ambience.

His hands smooth the hair behind my ears. It's such a small gesture, but it feels grander with what is to come. I lift his shirt slowly and he begins to take mine off. We both start undressing each other at a slow pace, leaving a trail of clothes covering the floor.

I can't think.

I can't breathe at the sight of him. He is perfect.

I tip my head towards the floor, suddenly feeling self-conscious of my body. I've always been nervous about how I look. I have stretch marks on my thighs and hips. I have extra fat in places.

"Look at me," Dustin commands, tipping my chin upward.

I look up to meet his blue-eyed gaze. The same gaze I've loved from the very beginning. I never realized that the color blue could be so dynamic; at times, they look to be as if I'm gazing into an endless body of water, but at this moment they glow like hot blue flames. "You're so beautiful." He breathes against my shoulder. The heat of his breath hovers over my skin. It lingers there. His fingers trail over my arms, to my hips, down my bare legs, leaving trails of goosebumps in their wake.

I slowly inch backwards towards the bed and he lays me down softly on the fluffy white duvet. He places his arms on either side of me and connects his lips with mine once again, but this time I can feel the longing.

"Do you have protection?" I whisper.

In one quick motion he grabs a condom from his nightstand drawer. I grab it from him, tearing the corner of the package. He groans against my touch.

As he slowly begins to enter me, I cry out in pleasure.

"Is this okay?" His voice comes out breathy.

"Yes," I moan loudly. The feeling of ecstasy begins to grow deeper. It entices me to embrace him in this way; I am drawn to him like a moth to flame. Blinded by lust filled air and the darkness of wooden paneled walls. Shadows flicker across our bodies from the stars. And it takes everything in me to control myself. I am on the precipice.

He continues his torturous pace. The smell of sweat mixed with his signature scent of pine and sandalwood permeates the air between us. My skin is clammy to the touch as I stare into his eyes, not daring to look away. The sight of him coming undone is too much for me to hold on any longer. "Dustin," I scream his name and shatter into a million pieces underneath him. Vibrating aftershocks of my body turn me into a jello-like state. We slump as one on our sides. I can still feel tingles where we were once joined. I breathe heavily as spots of sweat coat my forehead. Exhausted, unable to think or move from the spot.

"Where are you going?" I ask lazily. My eyes flutter closed. I'm so relaxed it's hard to keep them open.

"To take care of this. I'll be right back."

My eyes drift shut. Sleep overtakes my need to wait for him to return. I open my eyes once I hear his voice. "Let me clean you up." He brushes a warm cloth against my skin to clean me. The action makes me feel so much comfort; no one has ever done anything to care for me after. It's the difference between Dustin and the other guys I've been with in the past. He is special.

"Thank you," I whisper.

We both tangle under the covers. I rest my head on his chest, and I fall asleep to the sound of his breathing.

The words never leave my mouth, but I feel them all too well. I think I love him.

No. I know it.

Chapter 37

DUSTIN

L ast night was something I have never experienced before. Violet is an enigma. I've said it before, but now I can't help but feel the noun is perfectly her. This time in a different context though. I've been in relationships before, but never has anything felt like this. Like an enigma, she is difficult to understand. No, maybe I've got it all wrong. She's not an enigma; the mystery is the bond that we share. I've never ached to be near someone as badly as I ache to be with Violet. In every other relationship; surely, I've been happy, but not so utterly incapable of functioning without the other. When Violet and I are apart, I feel like a part of me is missing. She is the missing piece that I have been searching for years to find. Now that I've found her, I'm not letting go.

"Good morning sunshine." I smile at the beautiful woman walking down the stairs in my T-shirt. It fits halfway down her legs, draping like a dress. Damn, I can't believe she's mine.

"Good morning." She yawns, wiping the corners of her eyes in circle motions. Sardine hops from step to step after her. He's so tiny that the action is funny to watch. The cat follows her every move. Once I got up this morning he took my place snuggling on top of the covers next to her.

"Did you get enough sleep?" I ask. I grab two bowls from a wooden cabinet above the counter. I fill each of them with ripped up buttered toast and over easy eggs.

"Yes, that was the best sleep of my life." She looks down shyly at her hands. "I didn't have any nightmares. It's been years since I slept without one."

That thought stings as I think about the trauma she experienced at such a young age. Losing her parents in an accident changed her whole world. I want her to stay every night so that she never has to dread sleep again. So that she never has to wake up alone. Or experience another night of restless sleep.

"You should stay here every night then."

"I wouldn't complain." Her smile puts me at ease. I have a feeling she will be staying here from now on forever. If I have any say in it.

"Come eat. I made us dippy eggs." Her eyes glow in excitement. I love the way they light up. It takes everything in me not to pull her into my arms and carry her back to bed so that we can spend the day in bliss. But she needs to eat something. And I do too—I'm starving.

We eat in comfortable silence as the sunrise peaks through the windows, reflecting across the table. Dark hues of magenta and orange backfill the sky. The colors are so mesmerizing, but they are dull in comparison to her. We've only known each other a little over two months, but it feels as if we've known each other much longer. I think we're soulmates.

"Can I pick you up for lunch today?" I ask.

"Yes." Her eyes light. "What do you have planned?"

"I can't tell you, it's a surprise."

"You know I hate surprises."

"It's a good one I promise."

"Okay," She says hesitantly. "Do I need to change?"

"No, your overalls are perfect."

Chapter 38

VIOLET

Dustin picked me up at eleven, I was waiting eagerly in front of the NSSG. He was all smiles while we chatted in the car ride to the farm. When we first met, I thought he couldn't smile. Now it's all he ever does. My jokes are landing, his eyes crinkle with each one. I'm so wildly happy in his presence.

He opens the sliding barn door with a swift tug. The tractors and machines are all parked inside. "We can take the side-by-side." He says, motioning towards the vehicle. He opens a fridge to our left and pulls out a picnic basket. I look at the tractors and I get the sudden urge to ask.

"Can you teach me how to drive a tractor?" I have no clue where this is coming from. But it looks fun. I'd want to have a go at it.

"Yeah, why not? Want to learn now? We can take the bigger one there." He points in the direction of the big green one. "It's automatic."

"I was thinking something more on the lines of that one." I point to the one in the back, It's covered in a layer of dust. It's bright red and the smallest one in the barn.

"The farmall cub?"

"I think so, the smallest one."

He chuckles, "that one is a manual. It's harder to drive."

Does he think I can't handle the challenge?

Now that he said it, there's no way I'm backing down from the challenge. I want to learn how to drive that one.

"I can handle it."

"Okay, I think you can too. Just take it easy on the clutch, please. My grandpa would have my ass if we blew it out again. I did it one too many times growing up. It was his first tractor, he's sentimental about it."

"We don't have to take it out. I didn't know that."

"No we should for old times sake. Bertha needs to see some pastures again."

"You named it?" I laugh.

"Yes, when I was five. It stuck."

"I'll pull her out of here and we can drive it instead."

"Where are you going to sit?" I ask once it's sitting in front of the barn.

"I'll stand on the back."

"Where?"

"Where the implements attach."

"Is that safe?"

"It's safe enough. That's how my grandpa taught me." *Safe enough.* What does that mean? I'm starting to regret this idea.

He helps me onto the tractor. I'm feeling my confidence fleeting every moment. Being up this high with no clue what I'm doing is nerve racking. But I trust Dustin. I know he will make sure we're okay.

"Remember the brake is the pedal on your right. The clutch is on your left. The throttle is the little bar right here." He reaches his arm over me and moves the bar up, the tractor revs up higher. When he moves it back down it slows to an idle. "Got it?"

"Yes, that doesn't seem too bad."

"Good, we're going to start in first gear and stay in it, that way you can go slowly. We're going to the field to the far right. Just keep following it until you see apple trees."

"Okay."

"See the bar to the left of your legs, that's the gear shifter. You can wiggle it now. If it moves freely it's in neutral. Before we head off, which side is the brake and clutch?"

"The brake is on the right, and the clutch is on the left."

"Good."

He gives me a few more instructions on how to stop, how to slowly release the clutch so that it doesn't throw him off, how to shift into each gear and what to do on steeper ground. I paled when he talked about going up and down hills. Good thing where we're going is flat."

"I think you're ready. Press down the clutch, move the gear into first and slowly feather the pedal to release it."

I got this.

I try my best to let off the petal easily but it springs from my foot faster than I expected. We shoot forward, the motion makes him almost fall off.

"I'm sorry!" I shout.

"It's okay, you're learning." He chuckles. "We might lose our lunch. I almost threw it off. But it's a risk I'm willing to make."

I roll my eyes and laugh.

After we breeze through the pasture at a snail's pace, he instructs me on how to change into second gear, and third. We travel smoothly, the wind blows in my hair. His breath is hot against my ear. The sky is bright blue with thick white clouds. Everything is in full bloom, the trees bright green. I smile. And stop the tractor a few feet in front of the apple trees.

"Look at all the apples. I wish they were ready to eat!" I say, as he helps me off the tractor.

"You can have all the apples you want in the fall."

"I can't wait."

His eyes widen. "I forgot a blanket."

"That's okay. I like sitting on the grass and feeling it between my fingers. It's freeing. Grounding." I feel bad for derailing his plans. But it was worth it. Learning how to drive the tractor was nice. I trust Dustin, more than I have ever trusted anyone before.

He opens the wooden basket and removes two sandwiches, grapes, and some water.

"Thanks," I say, as he hands me my food. "It's really peaceful out here."

"It is. I want to spend the rest of my life here on this farm." He looks heavenward. "If you'd like, you can spend it here with me too."

It was a sweet thing to say. It warms my heart. But, I still have lingering doubts in the deep confines of my head. They have nothing to do with the man sitting next to me, looking at me like I'm his whole world.

"That would be nice." I say.

I just don't know if I deserve it.

"What do you have planned for the rest of today?"

"I'm going to check on the plants in the greenhouse. Then I'm heading straight to the Valley Harvest to interrogate Henry. I keep forgetting to talk with him; I've been so busy. I'm making it a priority today."

"Poor Henry."

"I'll take it easy on him, I promise."

"I can come with you. I'm sure my grandpa will be pissed. But I don't care. If you need me, I'll be there with you."

"No, I'm good. Please don't piss off George, I already broke their fine china. I don't need anything else to add to that list." She gives a half-suppressed laugh. "Besides, I need to do this on my own. Now that I know it's Henry the hard part is already figured out. You fulfilled your end of the bargain."

"I didn't even do anything."

"You helped me figure out who it was, that was more than enough."

Chapter 39

VIOLET

"Hi, Henry!"

"Good morning, Miss Vivi! Come in, have a seat." His smile beams at me when I knock on his office door. "Is that for me?"

"Of course it is. Olive whipped up an extra dark roast for you." His eyes crinkle with delight as he accepts the white paper cup and takes a huge gulp.

"Mmm. This is just what I needed this morning. To what do I owe the pleasure?"

I look down at my feet, suddenly feeling shy. I know this isn't my place, but curiosity is itching at my bones. I am dying to know why she wrote secret letters to him for so many years. Did they have a grand love, or did she hide these confessions without ever expressing her true feelings with him? Dementia is something that takes such a catastrophic toll on a person. She's still at an early stage, but it's hard to ask these questions. It hurts her to remember, and I can't stand making her upset. When I talk to her and she gets a frantic look in her eyes I know that she's pretending to recall something she doesn't. I don't want to be the cause of that. I'd rather ask Henry than make her upset or confused.

"Is everything alright Vivi, dear?" Henry's husky voice breaks me out of a trance.

"Yes, yes everything is alright. I had a few questions about this." I pull the notebook out of my purse and slide it onto the varnished wood desk, hoping to see a glimpse of recognition on his features. There is none, to my dismay.

Does he not know?

"What's that?"

"It's a notebook I found in the NSSG. It was Darcy's. She wrote entries almost every day to someone whose name starts with H." I keep a hold on the notebook as I continue, "I was wondering if that was you?" *I know it's you.*

"It has to be me. Darcy and I have been best friends since we were teenagers. Did you know we were as thick as thieves back in the day?" Henry's eyelids droop but a coy smile appears on his face. It's almost as if he's sad yet filled with love at the memory.

"I didn't know."

"If you want, I can tell you stories about us." I nod in agreement, eager to find out more about younger Darcy. "But first, can you read one of her entries? If it's not too personal; it's okay if you don't want to. I would love to listen to something she wrote years ago."

A huge grin tilts the corners of my mouth. "Of course, she said I could read them. I don't see why I couldn't read you at least some of them." I flip to one of the last pages choosing one that I haven't read yet and begin.

"Dear H,

I never knew what love was until I met you. Most people say it feels as if you are falling in love. But I don't want to fall into something that is so effervescently perfect. I'm trying to think of a word that could describe it. Float! I want to float into love. Just like butterflies appear to float through the air. Flapping their wings and flying so gracefully. A breathtaking creature that only lives for a few days. Prepossessing things like that don't last for eternity, but that's what makes it subjective. Love, though, defies all odds and lasts for eternity.

There are so many adjectives to describe what love entails. Just a word used to describe a feeling that is in your heart. Passion, kindness, belonging, bliss, forgiveness. There will never be enough ink or paper to express my longing for you. So that's why I'm delighted that I made the grand step of telling you how I feel.

When you told me you always loved me but were too afraid to say something I knew it in my heart we were always meant to be. There may have been reasons why I didn't follow this inkling, and why you kept quiet. None of that matters when we are free to be happy together once and for all.

With Love,
Darcy Burton"

I swipe back tears and look at Henry. His eyes are watery as well.

"So, you're together? I didn't know. I never read this one."

"Yes, not until a few years ago before she was diagnosed with dementia did I find out about how she felt."

"Why didn't you say anything?"

"She asked me not to say anything. Although, I'm not sure that was a good idea."

"Why didn't she want to say anything to me?"

"She didn't want you to ever feel as if you weren't her most important priority. You had no one left but her in your life. Darcy thought that it would hurt you more at the time. You have to understand what she did was what she thought was for your best interest. She loves you."

That, I know is true.

Chapter 40

Violet

I had to get out of there as fast as I could. I know why she kept this a secret from me for so many years. And why she kept it from Henry as well.

I caused my parent's accident and then I kept Darcy from years of being with her soulmate. She was always meant to be happy. Everything she does is selfless.

Henry's words keep ringing through my mind. *Not until a few years ago before she was diagnosed with dementia did I find out about how she felt.* She had to have been holding back from telling him for thirteen years. Now that she has dementia everything is wrong, so wrong. The years she does have left with him, will she even remember them as the disease progresses? No, most likely not. The thought aches in my bones.

How can I not ruin a relationship with Dustin too? He deserves way more than the shell of myself I am offering him. I only have a small part of myself to give, and what's left of that is broken. The more and more I think about it, the more I know I need to save him from the turmoil that is my life. I'll only bring him down with me.

After making it back to my shop, I spend the rest of the day filling flower orders, watering plants, and organizing inventory. My phone continues to vibrate in my pocket every few minutes during the day, but I can't bear to look at it. I know it's Dustin. I know that he cares. I know that I will let him down.

It's for the best.

Once afternoon rolls around, I slump on the couch dreading what I know is inevitable.

"Violet, are you okay? I was so worried about you, you weren't answering any of my calls or texts. Did something happen with Henry?" He looks so worried, and the sight makes what I am about to do hurt so much more.

"I'm okay."

"You're lying. I know you, darling. I can tell when something is wrong. Just tell me. I'm here for you." He grabs my hand in his.

I shake my head. "I—"

"Whatever is hurting you, we can get through it together. You're not alone anymore."

"That's the problem," I say shakily. "I don't think we can do this together. There's nothing forcing us to be together anymore. Now that the competitions are long over there's nothing forcing this. You have to focus on the farm, and I have my shop to run. There isn't time left for you and me." *I can't handle losing you if I get any more attached.*

I think I'm already too attached. It's going to ruin me regardless of the outcome.

"You know that isn't true. There will always be time for you and I."

"I can't do this."

"Yes, you can. What can I do? Why are you upset? I can take some of your hurt on my shoulders. I can take it all."

"I mess everything up, okay?"

"No, you don't." His expression softens.

"Yes, I do! I am the reason my parents are gone! I am the reason Darcy never went after Henry, her soulmate. She spent the past thirteen years of her life hiding her love for him because she didn't want to feel like she was putting anyone else above me. She thought I would feel abandoned. I'm going to ruin your life like I do with everyone else's. And I can't let that happen.

"You are not at fault for either of those things."

"I am though, you don't even know. I haven't told you. I've been too afraid to tell you." I pause, wishing the words I have to say never had to leave my mouth. "I made my parents late that day because I was too worried about how I looked. We were going on vacation, and I spent an extra hour worried about my hair. If I didn't make them late, we would have never been in an accident. Then to make things worse, I put my headphones in and ignored them the whole car ride. I don't even remember the last thing I said to them."

"That's not your fault. You were a kid; how would you know something like that would happen? You didn't." His voice softens.

"It is."

"No, it's not, and I'm never going to leave you no matter how much you try to push me away, dammit. I love you. Are you hearing me? I love you, Violet Tarynn Hart."

He loves *me?*

No. No. No. This isn't good. I've loved him way longer than I admitted it to myself. If I tell him that, he will never have a chance at what he really deserves. Someone who can give him everything, all of them. That someone isn't me.

"I—I'm sorry but I don't love you, I never have and I never will." I try my best to keep my voice toneless. I look down at the ground, fighting back tears that threaten to fall.

"You don't mean that." His voice is shaky.

"I do. Now go. Please." I don't want him to go. I am madly in love with him. And the thought of hurting him is devastating.

"I—"

"Just go Dustin." The defeated look that crosses over his face breaks me as he turns to leave.

Just like that, he's gone. He said he would never leave. But I said the only thing I knew that would make him.

Chapter 41

DUSTIN

It's been three days since I told Violet I loved her. It's also been the same number of days since she told me she didn't love me back. The thing is, I know she was lying. As she said it, she looked down at her feet. I knew instantly it was a lie. I had to give her some space to work things out with herself. So, I did the last thing I wanted to do and left. I walked out the door as I painstakingly listened to her sobs. It almost broke me to leave her in that condition. No, it did break me.

I regret it now.

I promised I wouldn't leave. There was nothing I could do or say to make her want me to stay in that moment. I know what she was doing: pushing me away. Like she always does. I did the only thing I thought I could, and that was to send Olive over to talk with her.

She assured me she would make sure she was okay. And I trusted that she would.

"Quit sulking over there and help me out," Mason calls from the other end of the bar.

"You really need to hire someone," I grumble as I continue collecting empty pitchers, plates, and glasses. Somehow Mason suckered me into helping out closing at Rooster's the past couple of days. Not that I'm complaining too much. At least I'm kept busy around the farm during the day and at night I spend the last few hours cleaning up the bar. Once I hit my bed every night, I'm so exhausted that I crash.

Through everything I have going on I still think about her every waking moment. I can't even bear to look at the damn cat. Violet and Sardine are both my undoing.

Everything around me reminds me of her. I can't even go for a run. The pond makes me think of the day we went fishing and the smile I saw return to her face. Don't get me started on her smile. The way Violet's smile lights up any room that she enters, confounds me. How she wears crazy outfits and doesn't give a damn about what anyone thinks of them. The way she is obsessed with watching *Shrek* relentlessly even though she's watched it so many times. The way animals gravitate towards her presence alone speaks of the warmness she carries. That green thumb of hers, nurturing any plant she touches. Hell, she even keeps orchids alive; that is an almost impossible feat. I am a fool, a fool in love. And it's killing me to be apart from her. I know she needs me but doesn't want to need me right now. So, she's cutting everyone off.

"Why do I need to hire someone when I have free help?" He chuckles.

"Fair point. I quit. Now you need to hire someone."

"Oh, come on man. I appreciate the help and you know it." He points an accusing finger in my direction. "When hay season comes around, I will be helping you out for days straight."

"And you're always good for it." I know damn well every year while I was gone, avoiding this place out of guilt, he was here helping my grandfather twice a year.

I bring a stack of dishes back to the sink and pile them in the spray station. Mason comes whipping through the door behind me carrying another stack. Once he places his dishes in the sink too, we enter the bar to finish cleaning off tables and mopping the floor. Mason looks at me and sighs. "She's going to come around eventually; hang in there."

"Do you think so?" I'm starting to feel skeptical that she really is anymore. It's been three days without so much as a word or text. I'm trying to give her the space she needs right now. But it's so difficult to know that she's suffering.

"Yeah, Olive thinks she will. So I would bet on it. They have a close-knit relationship."

"Thanks Mason."

"Anytime brother."

I really hope he's right. Right now, I'm starting to doubt she will ever come around again.

Chapter 42

VIOLET

Knock. Knock. Knock. The pounding on the front shop door is insistent and won't stop. I've been hearing it for the past five days. In the morning it starts and stops. In the evening it starts and stops. My phone flashes with a call from Olive. It habitually rings every morning around this time.

"You can't keep ignoring me!" she calls from the front door like a banshee. Although her voice is muffled, I can make out the words.

It's time for me to let her in.

I slump out of bed and pad my sock-covered feet into crocs. I slowly walk down the stairs to the front door, unlocking it and relocking it once she enters. I walk back up to my living room. The whole trek up the stairs I hear Olive huffing and puffing behind me. She is not happy with me. And I can't blame her one bit. I've been ignoring everyone the past five days, not even caring enough to open the shop for the day. I've been living in my bed reading romance novels to torture myself. Why does everyone else get a happy ending but me?

You did this to yourself, Violet.

Thank you, subconscious.

I plop back on the couch and make eye contact with Olive.

"You look like hell."

"Yeah," I mumble. I can't imagine what I look like to her right now. My hair hasn't been washed in days and it's sticking all over the place. There are books scattered on the counter and floor. Meanwhile, Fiona prances from book to book as if she's playing the floor is lava. At least she's having a good time.

"When's the last time you had a shower?"

"I don't know."

"Go take a shower. I'll make you something to eat." I shake my head left to right. I don't want to get in the shower because it will make me realize how badly I messed up. "Go, now!" Her aggressive voice comes out, and I begrudgingly head to the shower, sulking.

As I massage shampoo in my rat's nest of brown locks, I think about all the ways I messed up. The steam of warmth and fresh fragrances clear my head enough to really know that I screwed up.

I miss Dustin. I miss everything we were together. I miss his smile and warmth. His laughter. I miss Sardine. If I could come up with a way to get him to forgive me that would be great. That's the problem—everything that comes to mind is not good enough.

I can't think of any way to tell him I love him that will make up for what I've done. Saying it isn't enough. I need to show him how I truly feel.

If he will even forgive me.

I could send him flowers with a note saying sorry.

No. That's too corny. But men don't normally receive flowers so it might work. Nope. Not good enough.

Think.

Maybe I'll see what Olive thinks.

Once I got out of the shower and dressed into another one of Dustin's shirts, I made my way to the living room to find it completely sparkling clean. The aroma of frozen chicken tenders and boxed macaroni and cheese fills my nostrils. My stomach grumbles at the prospect of my favorite food. I've been a horrible friend too.

"Thank you." I smile shyly in her direction. "You made me one of my favorite foods."

"I did, because I know you need something to make you feel better. Mac and cheese is just what the doctor ordered." She places a steaming plate in front of me. "And you're welcome. Now let's eat so we can come up with a plan on how you're going to get Dustin back."

"Why do you think I'm planning to get him back?" I swear, sometimes she can hear my thoughts.

"We're sisters, of course I know."

"I'm sorry."

"Don't apologize to me. We need to work on apologizing to the right person."

"Let's get started," I mumble as I shove a huge fork full of food into my mouth.

Step one: eat something. Step two: make up the rest of the steps as I go.

Chapter 43

VIOLET

There are two things I knew I needed to do before I went to see Dustin. One, I need to visit my parents' graves. It's time. Two, I need to go see Darcy to work things out.

The stone before me reads, *In loving memory of Lily J. Hart & John A. Hart.* One stone, but for two people, forever together like they always wanted. "Hi Mom. Hi Dad. I know I should have been here more often. Who am I kidding, I should have come here in the first place. I haven't. It's not that I didn't love you. I loved you both more than everything in the world. More than life itself. I think about you both every single day. There's not a day that passes that I don't remember something you both liked or did. I was too afraid to come here because I didn't want to make it real. I couldn't face that you're truly gone and can't come back. I pray every day that I can go back and make a different decision that could have changed our trajectory. But I can't dwell in the past anymore. There's nothing to be done now. I need to focus on the future. Darcy taught me something and she's right. Sometimes in life you have to suck it up. She may have been talking about meatloaf, but it applies here too." I laugh quietly, knowing they would both get a kick out of Darcy's shenanigans. "I need to face what I've been avoiding for so long. I now know what true love feels like. Love is eternal like the love you both shared for each other. And we shared it with each other. It doesn't die when you do, it will always be there.

"I've needed closure for so long. I know it's not my fault we got into the accident. I was so young and dumb. I was more worried about my hair than being on time. That doesn't change anything; the drunk driver wasn't my fault. Sometimes things happen. Whether that be good or bad. I love you both. And now that I love someone else, I am pushing him away because I've been afraid of love. Not that I'm afraid to love. I'm afraid to lose it. Just like I'm losing Darcy slowly to an inevitable disease." I wipe my tears and hold the side of their gravestone.

"I need to go tell him how I feel; hopefully it isn't too late. I know you're watching over me. Laughing along with me, crying along with me. And that gives me hope. Here's to seeing each other more often."

I wipe another tear from the corner of my eye as I go to leave two butterflies land on their grave. I know it's them telling me they heard me, a sign that makes me finally feel at ease.

"I love you." And I swear I hear, "We love you too," in the whispers of the wind.

"I visited their graves today." I say, sitting across from Darcy.

"You did? Oh, honey I am so proud of the woman you have become."

"You are?"

"Yes. That had to take some guts to go there after all this time. I know it was too hard for you to go after so many years. But you needed to. And now that you have you can finally rest all of the blame you place on yourself."

"You're right."

"Now, why are you here? Go apologize to Dustin."

"How do you know?"

"*Sources,* remember? Anyways, what's wrong?"

"I know who H is. It's Henry."

"Oh my dear. I should have told you so long ago."

"Why didn't you?"

"I didn't want to hurt you. I needed you to think that I was never going to put anyone before you. You needed me. After time passed on it was easier to keep it from you than to tell you."

"I wouldn't have been hurt; I would have been happy you found someone."

"I know that now, but you have to understand I am sorry for keeping it from you, at the time I made a decision I felt was best."

"It's okay, I understand that you did what's best. You've done so much for me."

"I love you, Vivi. Now go get your man."

"Love you too, Darcy. I'm going right now."

"Good girl. I hope I get an invitation to the wedding."

I chuckle. Too soon for that, but let's hope he forgives me first.

Chapter 44

VIOLET

The drive to Dustin's place is anxiety ridden. My palms are sweaty, I'm itching all over and I know that this is long overdue. Now that I've stopped blaming myself for things that weren't my fault I feel as if a huge weight has been lifted from me. I need to apologize to him for everything I said. It's the last bit of weight holding me back. I miss him.

I knock on his door. I'm full of anxiety and it's like déjà vu all over again. It feels like it was only yesterday when I was knocking on his door to stay the night. In reality it's been a week.

I hear him pause the TV and walk to the door. He opens the door slowly looking as upset as I do. His stubble has grown so much since I've seen him last. I don't know what I was thinking he was going to do, but it wasn't this. He lifts me up into his arms and spins me around in a fast circle, then proceeds to tickle my armpit.

I start laughing because I can't control it. The pressure against my armpit sends me into a fit of giggles.

"What are you doing? You're crushing your gift."

"I missed your smile so much I had to do something about it." I was so stupid. He is the best thing I ever had, and I ran away. Like I ran away from everything else that was too hard to face. But this time I'm going to stay. That's if he wants me to stay.

"I forgive you," he says and kisses me softly on the lips.

What?

I am in disbelief.

"I had this whole speech prepared to beg you to forgive me. I even wrote you a letter," I say as he places me down.

"I already know you didn't mean it when you said you didn't love me."

"You do? How would you know that?"

"You were looking at your feet."

"And?"

"Every time you lie, or you are being shy you look at your feet." He sighs, looking at me. "And you weren't being shy."

"I didn't even realize I did that. Will you please accept your gift?"

"Yes, I would love to." He tugs me to sit on his couch with him.

"Here." I place a small snake plant in his arms.

"What's this?" He studies the plant and his eyebrows go up when he notices why it's so special. "Is this *the* pot?"

"Yes, it's the one I hit you in the head with when we first met. I still feel bad about that."

"You saved it..." His voice trails off. "I wouldn't change a thing about that day. When you hit me in the head it was a sign to wake up and realize what was right in front of me. And that was you."

"You're going to make me cry."

"Don't cry." He brushes his thumb against the side of my face. "No more crying, only laughing. Promise me."

"I can't make any promises but at least let me tell you what the letter said." I unfold the piece of paper and read it aloud, "I love you Dustin Cole Rhett. I've never loved someone as much as I love you. You make my heart beat so fast I'm afraid it might come right out of my chest. I love the way you can joke with me and the way it feels to be snuggled up against you. I love the way you constantly brush hair out of my eyes; it makes me feel butterflies every single time. I love the way you say positive affirmations to chickens. I love the way you bought a kitten that's named Sardine just because he looked at you the way Puss in Boots does to *Shrek*. I love that you help your grandparents and risk your life to set up a phone connection for them because you want them to be able to call someone if anything goes wrong. (Fingers crossed your grandfather doesn't find out you put it up there.) I love you so much. And I'm sorry for making you feel that I didn't. When I said we were a *fowl match* I was so wrong. We are an *eggs-cellent* match. Can you ever forgive me?"

"Oh, Violet. There's nothing to forgive. I never blamed you for anything." He pulls me in tighter against his chest. Dustin kisses me tenderly with so much passion it makes my heart ache. "I love you too."

This is where I belong. Safe in his arms. There's nowhere else I'd rather be than right here with him by my side.

Epilogue

DUSTIN

A year and a few months later

"Hello, Wife."

"Hello, Husband." Violet sings-songs as I tug her into me for a long overdue kiss. We had to sneak away for this time alone, because everyone was outside celebrating the Fourth of July and our wedding reception. I needed a few minutes of time with her. Without prying eyes.

Violet and I eloped a few months ago at a small courthouse. We were too eager to be married and didn't want to have a wedding. We spent the weekend at the Thornwood Cabins to have some time alone. Our quick *honeymoon* was spent rolling in the sheets, hiking trails, and having movie marathons. It was all I could have ever hoped for and more. Our real honeymoon is planned in a few months. We're going to Alaska to sight see and fish. It was something that Violet always wanted to do, and I couldn't think of anywhere else that I would rather be than with her. I can't wait to get away from everything and enjoy her company.

My family wasn't so happy with me when they found out we were already married without a wedding. After a few weeks of begging, we agreed to have some sort of celebration. So of course, Olive wanted to plan today for Violet, being the best friend/bridesmaid and all. I gladly agreed with the prospect, wanting nothing to do with party planning.

"Where are the lovebirds?" The buzz of conversation filters within the open door. Olive and Mason's voices echo into the open kitchen door.

"Coming!" Violet yells. Everything was set up between my grandpa's house and my A-frame. Blue and white bouquets of flowers that Vivi made are on each table. Four large tables dedicated to food line the side. Pepperoni rolls courtesy of The String Cheese, pastries from The Olive Bean, and a cookie table from Annie's Diner. Mason also brought drinks from Roosters Bar. Everything is perfect; I couldn't have asked for better friends to share this moment with.

The whole town was invited. Henry and Darcy sit together, smiling with loving glances at each other now that the whole town knows they are an item. My parents, sister, and Nolan are here.

Even Chelsea, Violet's new friend, came with her mother; they seemed to have made up after Violet talked to her.

Constance begins to walk up to us, and I grab Violet's hand. "Congrats on getting married. I'm so happy for you both." She adjusts her glasses to sit on her nose. "I would have thought by now you would have thanked me."

"What for?" I ask, having no clue what in the hell she's talking about.

"Oh, you know—" No, I don't know. Please enlighten me. "For rigging the name pulling at Rooster's Bar so that you and Vivi could be teamed together."

"You did what?" Vivi scowls, words clipped.

"You didn't think that was just a coincidence, did you? Oops." She shrugs as if it's no big deal. "It all worked out in the end. The gossip mill is behind everything, honey." She pats me on the back. She looks around her to make sure no one can hear her. "We're already *cooking* up something to get Olive and Mason together. Be prepared and keep it on the down low." Then she struts off.

"Did you know she rigged it?" Violet asks me.

"Nope. I had no idea." I had a feeling, but I'm not going to admit that now. Everything worked out the way I would have wanted it to.

"What's Helga doing here?" Violet asks, looking back and forth from me to her.

"I asked Mason to bring her; she's the main reason we're together. She deserved to munch on all of the scraps from the party."

"You're too much." She guffaws, pulling me into a hug.

"What the hell is that thing on my roof?" My grandpa's voice shouts above everyone else. There's a palpable tension in his tone. He stands up and points straight at the antenna I installed. The gaggles of people grow deadly quiet.

Shit. Shit. Shit. I am in deep shit.

Violet and I look at each other and burst out laughing. There will never be a dull moment around here. I don't know how I'm going to explain myself out of this one. "Are you thinking what I'm thinking?" I whisper under my breath.

"Yes. Run!"

Acknowledgments

To you reader. Thank you for giving my debut novel a chance. My dreams wouldn't be able to come to fruition without you. I am eggs-tremely grateful that you took a chance on my first ever novel! (Sorry had to add that pun.) I hope you loved Dustin and Violet's story as much as I enjoyed writing it. I've spent two years trying to come up with the perfect way to put it all together and I can't believe I finished it.

To my ARC readers. I have absolutely no words. The amount of people that signed up from Threads, Instagram, and TikTok was incredible. There were 378 of you that responded to my google form. I'm blown away that so many of you thought my book sounded good. So thank you from the bottom of my heart.

To Leilani Dewindt—my copy line and development editor. Thank you for helping me with flow, plot development, and giving me your honest feedback. It was so scary sharing my novel with someone and you were so kind and professional!

To Mom Mom, Pops, and Shannon—thank you for being my alpha readers and the first eyes on my novel. Thank you for inspiring some of my characters. And helping me with grammar, book name ideas, cover ideas, etc.

To my best friend Hannah, thank you for listening to me ramble on and on about my book ideas. And for always being so excited for me. It means so much.

To my husband, thank you for showing me what a friends to lovers trope looks like in real life. And for always supporting my crazy delusional dreams.

About the Author

Sarah Madeline lives for small town romances and swoon wor-thy, tension filled moments. She fills her pages with laughter and happily ever afters. She resides in small town Pennsylvania with her husband, miniature dachshund, cat, and eighteen chickens. Hopefully adding some goats to her family soon. When she's not writing, you can find her reading in front of a warm fire, fishing, baking, or gardening.

Email: sarahmadelineauthor@gmail.com
Instagram: @sarahmadelineauthor
TikTok: @sarahmadelineauthor
Goodreads: goodreads.com/author/show/54572302.Sarah_Ma
deline

www.ingramcontent.com/pod-product-compliance
Lightning Source LLC
Chambersburg PA
CBHW020418110726
47899CB00006B/2036